Hero...

Heroine

a novel by

D. Mitchell

Q-Boro Books
WWW.QBOROBOOKS.COM

An Urban Entertainment Company

ISBN-13: 978-1-933967-63-9
ISBN-10: 1-933967-63-3
LCCN: 2007940330

First Printing October 2008
Printed in the United States of America

10   9   8   7   6   5   4   3   2

This is a work of fiction. It is not meant to depict, portray or represent any particular real persons. All the characters, incidents and dialogues are the products of the author's imagination and are not to be construed as real. Any references or similarities to actual events, entities, real people, living or dead, or to real locales are intended to give the novel a sense of reality. Any similarity in other names, characters, entities, places and incidents is entirely coincidental.

Cover Copyright © 2008 by Q-BORO BOOKS, all rights reserved. Cover layout/design: Candace K. Cottrell; Photo: Frank Antonio
Editors: Melissa Forbes, Candace K. Cottrell

Q-BORO BOOKS
Jamaica, Queens NY 11434
WWW.QBOROBOOKS.COM

Acknowledgments

I would like to thank GOD for many the blessings he's given me. I want to thank my mother Wanda Henson for making me the man that I am. I want to thank my wife Natalie for standing by me good and bad. I want to thank my children, Wayne, Chinelle, and Dariyana for supporting me. I want to thank my brothers Mykell and Ryan, sister Robbyn, and stepfather Michael Henson for their support and advice.

I'd like to thank my mother-in-law May Green, brother-in-law Ricky Dixon, father-in-law and mother-in-law Lewis Dixon and Elizabeth Myles for supporting me.

I want to thank Candace Cottrell for all of her help, patience, and belief in me. Thanks to Mark Anthony for looking out for me.

Thanks to everyone who purchased *Chaos In the Capital City* and everyone who purchased this book.

Thank you very much,

D. Mitchell

Chapter One

Metaphorically Speaking

The darkness of the room wasn't half as frightening as the piercing light or the thunder that accompanied it. The light invaded the room, but the darkness controlled it. Samara sat on the edge of the bed unfazed by the brightness or the deafening noise that seemed to rattle the windowpanes. The flashing light created a black and white picture of a grief-stricken woman with an assault rifle resting at her side.

The storm continued both outside and inside. Samara sat in the darkness as the tears welled in her eyes until the unthinkable happened. A lone tear escaped and raced down her face. It was followed by another until tears flowed freely down both sides of her nose. She had only cried twice in her life since the age of two, but now she was powerless to stop the steady stream of tears that fell onto her shirt.

Samara was fighting so many battles with so many different enemies that she didn't know who was who, or whether she was coming or going. During the past week she had been jailed, shot, and had watched her best friend get gunned down. On top of that her name had been slandered across the nation as a heinous criminal. Things were so bad that there was only one thing that could make everything better—death.

She couldn't believe that she was contemplating suicide. Her father would've killed her if he knew the thought had crossed her mind. He had spent more than half of her life preparing her for the tough times. Those times were destined to come with the purpose he presented for her, and now that the time was at hand, she wasn't sure she could handle it.

The phone rang, and before it paused to ring a second time, an AR-15 rifle was pointed at the phone, and Samara was on her feet and ready to fire. She quickly rotated the gun from the phone to the door before the phone continued to ring. The phone rang a second time. She raised the gun to eye level to get an accurate shot. The phone rang a third time and stopped.

Samara held her stance with her gun trained on the door. She held her position for about two minutes, looking at the bottom of the door, making sure the little bit of light that entered was uninterrupted.

Boom! The thunder crackled and nearly scared the life out of her. Another pound of pressure on the trigger would have sent bullets flying. She slowly proceeded to the door. Lowering the gun to her midsection, but still aiming it at the door, she peeked through the peephole. No one was in sight.

Had someone been on the other side of that door, that someone was getting shot. Any attempt to open or knock on the door would have resulted in bullets going through it. No discussion or identification was necessary. Anything they had to say could be said to their creator. The police could do the identifying later. Her motto was to shoot first and let that be her final answer.

The simple ringing of the phone had somehow saved her. It was like an alarm clock waking her out of a bad dream. Gone was the despair and self-pity that had consumed her a few moments before. Her Darwin-like survival instincts took hold, and she was back on track.

Samara couldn't believe that she had been so weak. She had a lot of problems, and instead of crying about them or letting them dictate her actions, she would be more proactive. Her daddy told her that there would be stretches where she would have to be a different person, and that time had come.

After she was assured that no one was putting her or themselves in danger, she headed toward the bathroom. She stopped at the sink with the wall length mirror that sat just outside the bathroom. She looked back to the entrance door to make sure there weren't any shadows, and then Samara flipped on the light to the small room adjacent to the bathroom.

She looked into the mirror at herself and saw two people at the same time. One of those people's eyes were red from crying and staying awake the past sixteen hours. The other looked like an assassin with the large caliber rifle in her right hand. She placed the rifle on the six-foot-long counter/sink area. Turning on the water, she caught the stream in both hands and used it to rinse her face.

The lightning flashed again, illuminating the rest of the hotel room. Samara had been transient for a couple of days prior to her stay there. An attempt on her life had rearranged her home from wood and stone to ashes. Her life from day to day was filled with uncertainty. All that she had accomplished was being undone right before her eyes.

If only her father were there. She needed his advice

and counseling. Just to hear his voice would make everything OK. But she doubted that she would hear his voice again in this lifetime.

Her father contacted her at least once a week whenever he was away, wherever he was, be it in a faraway country or in a jail cell. She hadn't heard from her father in more than a year, and with the life he lived, she had to presume he was dead. After she didn't hear from him for a month, she was worried. After two months she was ready to cry, but refused to do that. After six months with no contact, no postcard or letter, she knew the only answer could be the one she didn't want to face.

After thinking about her daddy, tears started to form in her eyes. Then she imagined him standing beside her. She immediately held back those tears. Samara could see the smile on her daddy Rufus's face. She could hear his easygoing manner telling her, "Everything is goin' be OK. We'll get through it. I'm always with you."

She loved how smooth and confident he was. With his backing she never had to worry about anything. He was easygoing, but prohibited crying, not just in his presence, but ever. He taught her to be mentally and physically tough, and now she would have to use both of those skills to survive and maintain her sanity.

Samara grabbed the rifle and returned to the bed. The sound of the rain beating on the window provided some tranquility for her as the thunder and lightning subsided. She sat on the bed and starting thinking about how she could right the wrongs done to her and reclaim her life and her work.

Out of nowhere came a knock, knock, and a light kick at the bottom of the door. Samara jumped off the bed, leaving her rifle on it. Another light kick, knock, kick at the door. Her heart began to beat so hard and fast she could feel it in her throat. Then there was a kick, kick, knock, knock, and a pause before a final kick. She rushed toward the door, but stopped midway. Slowly she moved back to the bed and retrieved the rifle before returning to her position by the door.

With her gun pointing at the door, she looked through the peephole. On the other side of the door was a man with both hands in the air, looking at the hole.

"Sammie, we need to talk," the unidentified man said. Samara moved her finger from the ready position of the trigger guard to the trigger. The only person who was allowed to call her Sammie was her dad. She would tolerate being called Sam or Mara or Maury, but would quickly rebuke anyone who called her Sammie, including her mother. The only reasons the man wasn't full of bullets were because he did the knock that only her and her father knew, and he called her Sammie.

"Name?"

"The pirate," the man responded.

"Where are you from?"

"Hell! Just visiting."

After removing the locks, Samara quickly moved away from the door.

"Slowly enter with your hands in the air in front of you." The man complied. When he entered she thought this man might have been her father. She wasn't sure if there really was a resemblance, or if she just wanted him to be her father so badly that she had conjured the resemblance in her mind. "Close the door and strip down to your underwear and socks," Samara demanded.

"I don't even know you like that," he joked with Samara. She raised the gun eye level. He hastily removed his clothing. Rufus had already instructed the man on all the things he needed to do to see Samara and live—from the special knock, to the code words, to compliance with any order she gave. She wasn't nearly as ruthless as her father, but she was by no means above killing anything she perceived as a threat.

"Take your pants and turn the pockets inside out," Samara ordered. The man complied. "Turn you pants upside down and shake them. Shake your shirt." After complying with both demands, she continued, "Put your clothes on and sit on the bed." The man put on his clothes and sat on the bed.

Samara had a very somber look on her face. She went and sat on a chair about six feet away from the man. The rifle followed the man from the time he entered the door until she sat opposite him. With her lie detector pointed directly at the man, she asked, "Where's my dad?" The man took a long pause before answering.

"He's OK. He's into—" She abruptly cut him off.

"I didn't ask how. I asked where."

"He's close, very close. He told me first and foremost to apologize for not contacting you and that he'll explain when he sees you. The reason he sent me to talk to you instead of himself is because he's caught up in something and he believes he's being watched. He wanted to let you know he's here now and would take care of things."

A light smile had formed across Samara's face, which was previously void of any emotion at all.

"When and where will I see him?"

The man reached into his pocket. Samara clutched the gun, advancing a warning his way. He lifted his free hand in submission and slowly extracted a small piece of paper. She pointed to the floor with her gun. He dropped the paper. She nodded her head toward the door. The unidentified man slowly rose and headed for the door.

"What's your name?" Samara asked. He pointed to the paper and kept moving. She stood as he prepared to open the door. He walked through the door as the lightning illuminated the room. He closed it firmly and the sound of the thunder accompanied it.

Samara walked over and picked up the paper. The paper had the meeting place and time, written in a code her father had taught her. On the back of the paper was the name Wayne, which she assumed was the man's name. A huge smile formed across her beautiful face when she thought about seeing her father for the first time in nearly a year and a half. He couldn't have come back at a better time.

Chapter Two

Loosen Up

Four months earlier

It was a lovely spring day in the city. The temperature hovered around seventy degrees and the gentle breeze had many people mesmerized. The break from Old Man Winter came suddenly, and the pleasant weather had caused everyone from the very young to the elderly to come out and bask in the beauty of it. Even the young guys from the underworld relaxed over by the basketball courts, shooting around and talking about the NBA playoffs.

Samara sat on the bench with much more on her mind than the carefree play of the children or the adults shooting the breeze. She was set to graduate from Howard University in less than a month, and her only concerns were where her father was, and if he would be able to make her big day.

Samara hadn't talked with her dad in a year, and she knew the odds of him coming to her graduation were slim to none. In fact, she thought hearing from him again was just as unlikely. But knowing the strength of her father and the strength he instilled in her, she had to hold out hope. Although that hope was diminishing by the day.

Of course, her mother would be there, even though she wished that Samara would have attended one of the three Ivy League schools that had accepted her. Princeton even offered her a full scholarship, but Samara declined. The only reason she applied to those schools was as part of a social experiment. She applied to five upper echelon schools, listing her straight-A GPA and her top-five percent SAT scores at all the schools. She didn't list her all-American track or basketball experience on two of her applications, and the only schools that did not extend her an invitation to attend were the two on whose application she did not list her athletic achievements. Her point was proven. The schools only cared about black people who were athletes, and not about their scholarly achievements.

As Samara sat on the bench worrying about her father, a large, late model Mercedes Benz pulled up. Exiting the vehicle, a tall, light-skinned pretty boy strolled over to the bench Samara sat on. She instantly recognized Craig, the starting freshman point guard for the MEAC conference champions, the Howard University Bison. He had women chasing him from one side of the campus to the other.

Craig had noticed Samara awhile ago, but wasn't sure about her. The beautiful, fair-skinned woman that he had never seen wearing makeup was by far one of the most attractive women he had ever laid eyes on. After he asked around about her, he learned that she had not had a boyfriend since she attended the school. On top of that, she was a starting basketball player. The combination led him to believe that she was just not interested in his gender. But every time he saw her, she stopped him dead in his tracks.

"Are you OK?" Craig asked, taking a seat next to her.

"I'll be all right," Samara responded.

"Yeah, I know that. Is there anything I can do to make it better?"

She pointed to the car, and he smiled. "That door you opened on the fancy automobile of yours"—he nodded with a slight grin—"open it again, get in, and drive away," she said with a smile that disappeared a split second after her last word. Craig's face turned sour.

"Damn. What's all that for? You're over here looking sick in the face and I try to help you out and get all that extra?"

She sighed. "Look, Craig,"—he smiled at her acknowledgement— "I've got a lot on my mind and there's nothing you can do about it except get on my nerves. I just don't feel like being bothered right now."

Craig immediately got up and headed straight for his car. He got in, slammed the door, and sped off.

Samara stared blankly into the sky, wondering if her lifelong dream of establishing a community center would work out. Seeing the desperate situation of the black youth in the city made her cringe. How low some of her people had slid was bad enough, but to see the future generation's regression made her sick. There hadn't been a strong black leader the likes of Marcus, Malcolm, or Martin for a generation or two, and Samara was desperately seeking to fill that void. Unfortunately, her father taught her the by-any-means-necessary approach preached by Malcolm and practiced by the Black Panthers.

As Samara sat on the bench in deep thought, she noticed Tonya walking toward her. Tonya, a friend since childhood, was as close to Samara as a sister. They were set to graduate together, and Tonya was very excited. But the look now on Samara's face worried her, and wore down that enthusiasm.

"Maury, what's wrong, girl?" Tonya asked.

Samara shook her head.

"Nothing. I just hope my dad is able to make it to the graduation."

Tonya looked away as she felt tears begin to fill her eyes. She knew how important Rufus's appearance at the graduation was to Samara. And although they were close, Samara rarely talked to Tonya about her father. After seeing Samara depressed most of her senior year, she finally got Samara to tell her what was wrong. She thought her daddy was in a bad situation and she didn't think she would see him again.

Tonya choked back the tears. She had to be strong for her friend. If she were to break down, it would only make a bad situation worse for Samara.

"Girl, he'll be there. We'll just have to pray on it."

"Yeah, I guess so. God is the only one who can bring him there."

Tonya, sensing that their conversation wasn't going in the right direction, proceeded to switch gears.

"Was that Craig I saw you over here talking to?" she asked with a slight smile.

Samara pursed her lips and said, "Uhm hum," nonchalantly.

"And what were y'all talking about?"

"Basketball," Samara said flatly.

Tonya burst into laughter. Samara finally lightened up and got a light giggle out of the situation.

"Whatever. Girl, you know that when we walk across that stage we'll both be receiving degrees in psychology.

I hope you don't think mine is a fake. I saw the way he sped off, and judging from the attitude you have, you probably shooed him away."

"Damn, girl, are you sure you want to be a social worker? You should be a shrink or something," Samara replied, and they both laughed.

"I know he likes you. He's been asking around about you." She paused for a second. "Maury, he's one of the finest men on campus and an athlete, and I bet you could care less, right?" Samara smiled.

"He is, but I don't have time. Besides, you know I don't like light-skinned, curly-haired, pretty boys." They laughed. "I'm not trying to be one of his groupies."

"Girl, I've been telling you a long time now that you need to loosen up. If it is not about academics, athletics, or martial arts, you don't have time. You need to get you some to get all that frustration and extra energy up out of you." They both enjoyed a nice laugh together.

"Whatever, Tonya. My parents raised a lady."

"Right. A lady who I've never seen cry, can defend herself better than a lot of men, and is always armed. Well, Ms. Lady, I'm sure they didn't teach you to play with those toys you use to help you relax either."

They giggled like schoolgirls a little while longer before Samara noticed an early model '80s Chevy Caprice with dark tinted windows pull up. All the young men on the basketball court stopped everything they were doing and stared at the car. Samara opened her purse and depressed the button releasing the safety on her .380 caliber handgun before rising from the bench.

"Come on, girl," Samara said, helping Tonya up from the bench. "Let's get these kids away from here before they start that bullshit."

"Y'all need to get these kids out of here," Samara

said to the young adults charged with watching them. The people basically ignored her and continued on with their conversations. Samara and Tonya quickly moved to the children's play area, about twenty yards away from the basketball court, and began to usher the kids away. The parents and guardians of the children immediately took issue with them removing the children, who were between the ages of five and nine, from the play area.

"Hey! What the hell are you doing?" one lady in her early twenties asked as she approached the two. Samara simply pointed at the car with the dark tints and continued moving the children away from the area.

Just as Samara pointed to the car, two young men exited the vehicle. One carried an AK-47. The other carried a MAC-10. The two immediately opened fire with their weapons set on automatic, and flooded the basketball court with countless rounds. The young men on the court scrambled away from the hail of gunshots. Many were tagged as they attempted to flee. It was the last thing Samara saw of the scene as she, Tonya, the children, and the adults watching them all fled.

Chapter Three

My Brother's Keeper

It was just a week before Samara was set to graduate from Howard when she decided to go see her little brother Marcus Calvin, also known as MC. He hung out in the Fairfax Village neighborhood, which was just a few blocks from the Hillcrest single-family home he grew up in. MC had been a part of a gang since his early youth, despite the positive direction provided by both his parents.

Samara pulled up on her brother hanging out with a few of his boys on Thirty-eighth Street early in the afternoon. He walked away from his friends to greet his sister.

"What's up, big sis?"

"Nothing much. How are you?"

"Just trying to maintain, Sam. I'm just trying to maintain."

"Maintain what, Marcus?" Samara asked, obviously annoyed at his blasé answer.

"Life."

"Whatever. You're still out here bullshitting with your

friends and you call that maintaining. Look, I told you that I'm opening up the center next week. I got a full-time position for you."

"Oh, yeah. What am I gonna be doin'?" Marcus looked enthusiastic.

"You're going to be a youth counselor," Samara said. He nodded approvingly.

"What's the pay looking like?" he asked.

"I'm going to start you off at thirteen dollars an hour. That's a little over five hundred a week, before taxes. But the job comes with a catch."

Marcus shook his head. He wasn't happy with the catch, but he figured it was coming, knowing his sister.

"First you have to take these classes and get your GED," Samara said. Her brother's face lightened up some. "Second, and more importantly, you have to stop running the streets."

Marcus knew that was coming, but he also didn't really want to hear it. He sighed.

"What?" Samara asked, challenging him.

"I ain't running the streets," he replied.

"What exactly do you call it then?"

Marcus didn't immediately respond as his attention became fixated on a slow-moving, mid '80s Cadillac Deville that was traveling down the block. Samara took note of the car as well. She took a quick glance across the street and saw the same threatening stares coming from her brother's friends at the car. The car picked up speed and left the area.

Marcus turned his attention back to his sister.

"What were you saying?"

"Who was that?" Samara asked, ignoring his question.

"Nobody," MC replied. He was met with a powerful, piercing stare that was more intimidating than the one he was used to receiving from his mother. Samara didn't say another word, but waited impatiently for the answer she knew had better be forthcoming.

After a moment, MC took a deep breath and answered. "We're beefing."

"That much is obvious. My questions are with whom, and for what?"

"We got into it with some niggas at the club last night. My friends think it was those niggas from MLK. That's what we were discussing before you came."

"How serious is the beef? Did y'all just exchange words? Was there a fight? Did someone get stabbed or shot?"

"All of the above except no one got shot, only shot at." Samara shook her head.

"Do you see what I'm saying? This is the type of bullshit that I be talking about." Samara shook her head again as she thought about the situation. MC dropped his head like a kid who was waiting to be scolded. "Are you armed?" she asked. He didn't even look up when he shook his head again to indicate that he was not. "What! You have people coming to look for you, you don't know who they are or what they look like, and you don't have a weapon to protect yourself or at least deter them from coming through and lighting y'all's dumb asses up? You have to be kidding me."

"Sis, I didn't even go with 'em last night. I was out with one of my girls. I didn't find out about this until this morning."

"I thought 'we' went to the club last night," Samara replied, a little stunned by his statement.

"We being the crew," MC responded matter-of-factly.

Samara looked away for a second. It was a last ditch effort to prevent herself from smacking the hell out of her little brother. She calmed down just enough to think about the fallout of her embarrassing him in front of his friends.

"Look, Marcus, you don't even understand where you are. You're about to go jail or be killed over a beef you didn't have anything to do with. One of your boys could have felt on the wrong girl's ass. Someone may have stepped on somebody's shoes or whatever the hell happened. Regardless of what happened, it was not enough to be putting your life in immediate danger."

Just as Samara finished her statement three young men caught the attention of Samara, MC, and his friends, who were a little farther up the street. Samara was about to ask who the young men were, but the looks on their faces, along with their determined rough and rugged strut made their identity and intentions plainly obvious.

Samara stuck her hand in her purse, releasing the safety on her .380-caliber handgun. The young men were about forty yards away. At that range she could hit them, but her accuracy would be marginal. She considered firing some shots at them from that distance, which would force them to return fire from a distance from which they probably could not hit a parked dump truck.

While Samara was caught up in the game plan of offense and defense, she forgot about her primary concern—getting her little brother out of harm's way. After a moment, her thoughts returned back to her brother.

"Come on, Marcus," Samara said, pulling him by the arm. He snatched his arm away.

"Aren't you strapped?" he asked.

"What?" His question caused her to lose focus for a split second. "You know I am, but I'm not getting caught up in this bullshit." The young men were about thirty yards away and closing fast. "I'm a professional. I don't have time for these kid's games that you and your friends play."

The young men were about twenty yards away. At that range she could tag all three of them without having to reload.

The more she thought about it, the more frustrated she became with the situation. Because of her brother they were in more danger with less space and time to make a better choice than when the young men first entered the scene.

"Stay here," Samara said to her brother with a very stern look. "If guns come out, you get away from here. You can't help us without a gun and we might get hurt trying to protect you. Do you understand?" MC nodded and Samara immediately headed straight for the young men.

MC's friends immediately began to follow her down the sidewalk to confront the young men. Feeling their presence behind her, she turned halfway around and waved them off.

"Stay right there. I got this." She continued walking toward the young men until they were about ten feet away.

"Hold on, fellas," Samara said to the young men with her arms and hands stretched out in front of her. A big kid named Jo-Jo, who was in the middle of the three, pushed her aside.

"Get the fuck out the way," he said. She rolled right around the young man to his left and before they could take another three paces, Samara had a vice grip on the young man's neck with her left arm and a gun to his head with the right. The two young men were stunned by the sudden change in situation.

"If you breathe too hard, it'll be your last breath,"

Samara whispered in Jo-Jo's ear. "If you think you can overpower me, what little brain you have will be on the sidewalk before your body meets up with it." Jo-Jo put up no resistance. MC got up and started walking toward them. His friends joined him.

Jo-Jo's friends were wide-eyed. They didn't understand what was going on or how it had happened so suddenly. Their plan was to come on the block and blast. It took them nearly ten seconds before they regained their bearings enough to reach for their guns.

"I wouldn't do that," Samara said. Before the young men could draw their weapons, they heard two rapid click-clacks, the sound of bullets being loaded into chambers. They turned to see a 9 mm Beretta and .40-caliber semi-automatic handguns staring them in the face. "Put your weapons on the ground." The young men did as they were instructed. MC picked up both guns.

"I'm going to turn you loose now. You be still. No sudden movements," Samara said to Jo-Jo. She slowly released him and felt his waist for a gun with her left arm. She removed the gun and moved in front of them where MC and his friends stood. "Y'all back up a little," Samara said to the young men. They complied. "Put the guns away." MC and his friends did as they were told. MC had two guns at his waist with his arms folded across his chest like he was an enforcer. Samara shook her head. She placed her gun and Jo-Jo's gun in her purse.

"Look, fellas," Samara continued, "I don't know how this beef started, and I don't really care. We need to get together and talk about it under different conditions. Every time something happens that we don't like, we run and grab our guns and put someone's mother on the front row of a funeral home crying her

eyes out. If you have problems, let's solve them the organized way. I know where a field is for football, a gym
for basketball, and a boxing ring if you need to handle
it like that. But there's a better way than someone
dying and you being stuck in jail for the rest of your
life. To hell with what you see in the movies or in the
streets, because that shit ain't cute."

"What are you, a reverend or something," Jo-Jo asked.

"Not at all. I'm someone who loves you. I love you
even though you came here to kill my brother and his
friends. To be truthful, though, if any shots were fired,
all love would have been lost. I want y'all to be what
God intended you to be—powerful beyond measure. I
know you are, but you're just using that energy for the
wrong purpose. You don't have to be a drug dealer and
a killer to be somebody or get respect. All you have to
do is be a man."

All the young men stood there and absorbed Samara's words. Out of nowhere the Cadillac returned.
The driver, wondering why he hadn't heard any gunshots yet, stopped the car right beside the small crowd.
Samara flipped both guns on the car's driver in an instant. A few seconds later MC and his friends drew
their guns. The young man driving the Cadillac sped
off.

"Look at this bitch-ass nigga. Y'all show guns and he
speeds the fuck off. Just leaves his boys out here to
die," Jo-Jo said. They all got a light laugh off the incident.

"Fellas, let's handle this another way," Samara said.
"Let's go bowling or something."

"What's your name?" Jo-Jo asked.

"Samara, but I go by Maury."

"Well, Maury, you're a bad motherfucker. I would
never think someone as pretty, and sexy, and sophisti-

cated looking as you would be that good with a gun.
After I pushed you—and I apologize for that—you
could have killed us all before we knew what hit us.
I'm looking at you one second, turn to look at our car,
and less than a second later I turn to look at you and
see two guns pointed at the car. You're on a whole different level." He paused a second before continuing.
"You got some bodies, don't you?"

Samara looked away as if ashamed before facing him
again.

"Damn," Jo-Jo said, reading into her lack of an answer and facial expression. "Well look here, Maury,
I'm tired of dealing with these young hookers with
nothing on their mind. I need a real woman. You got a
boyfriend?" Samara smiled.

"I got a mission and I'm married to it. You can have
a real woman, but you have to get your mind right.
Come get in this job training program I got and step
your game up. Legal money lasts. That stuff y'all do
doesn't. Come to my center and let me show you a better way. That goes for y'all too." She directed her last
statement to MC and his friends.

"Give us the information and we'll be there," Jo-Jo
said. Samara handed all of them cards, including her
brother.

"All right, Maury, we're gone, but can we get our
hammers back?" Jo-Jo asked.

She pulled out Jo-Jo's gun, released the magazine,
and removed the round from the chamber. Samara
turned to her brother.

"Take out the clips and remove any rounds in the
chamber." MC was hesitant, but Sam shot him a look,
and all hesitation dissipated. Samara and MC handed
back the guns and the young men turned to leave.

"We're coming to your center, and not to take over

like we usually do. And I love you, too, Samara, and it's not just physical attraction. I love you for trying to make a difference even if it meant putting your life on the line to do it. There aren't many real men who would do that, let alone a woman. I love you for that."

Samara felt a hot flash take over her body. She could see that Jo-Jo had potential to be a leader, but his words had somehow, in an instant, turned her on. She couldn't even reply. She blushed and nodded in agreement, and the young men walked away.

Chapter Four

Graduation

Samara stood in the hallway with butterflies in her stomach. She was rarely nervous about anything, taking whatever came her way in stride, but the prospect of seeing her beloved father for the first time in more than a year fueled her anxiety. She was aware that her dad knew how important this day was to her. There was no question that Rufus would destroy a city block and/or murder dozens of people rather than disappoint his daughter. So it would seem death would be the only thing to stop him from showing up.

"Girl, I'm glad you're not standing here looking all sad today," Tonya said to her best friend. Even though their last names were separated by more than half the alphabet, the two managed to stand side by side because of their designations as valedictorian and salutatorian with Samara receiving the former honor.

Samara gave a hesitant, anxiety-filled smiled. Looking into her face, Tonya could see that Samara was nervous.

"Girl, I've been praying."

"It's goin' be OK," Tonya said, putting her arm around Samara.

All of the honorees marched down the aisle to their seats opposite the stage. Samara strutted down the aisle, scanning all sections for her father. She saw her mother and brothers, but no sign of her father.

Everyone took their seats and listened to the introduction. Samara hadn't given up yet. She pulled out a pair of binoculars and scanned the crowd again thoroughly, to the ire of her fellow graduates and some of the faculty who noticed her. In the upper section she spotted a man who looked just like Rufus, except he was about twenty to thirty years younger. The man beside him was too old to be her father, and he kept looking down at a program or something around the time she noticed him. She scanned the crowd a second time to no avail. After Samara didn't see her father, she put the binoculars down and zoned out.

Her anxiety-filled face quickly turned blank and despondent. Out of nowhere tears welled in her eyes. Tonya noticed and tried to grab Samara's shoulder to console her, but Samara refused the comforting touch. She recovered quickly and held back the tears without a single one escaping her eyes. She sat there emotionless, ignoring everything that was going on at the graduation.

To console herself she started to relive her memories of her father. All they had planned hinged on this moment in her life, graduating from an HBCU. It was a little divergent from the plans her father had for her, but he respected her decision and direction. He was glad that she had changed course from the life he taught her. The last thing in the world he wanted for daddy's little girl was for her to become a murderer, but he saw in her what he hadn't seen in either of his sons.

She recalled the story her father had told her that would ultimately change their destinies. Samara's grandfather had haphazardly started something he thought was destined to make an impact on the country's history. Using one of the most effective practices of mankind, murder would affect change, he believed.

Her grandfather, MC Bowser, had watched as his brother Sam hung from a tree for severely beating a white man in Depression-era Greenville, South Carolina. The white man's offense was cursing Sam over an incident in which Sam rebuked some white kids for harassing his little sister.

Sam never liked the whole second-class citizen situation and was always testing the system. His parents had warned him many a time about his attitude and knew it was only a matter of time before he came up missing or found hanging from a tree, but Sam was too proud to care.

"Boy! I tol' ya once 'for, not ta say a word ta dem kids," the white man said to Sam.

"Look her'. I ain't no boy. Ya tell dem dern kids ta min' der mannas when they be talkin' to my sista," Sam replied.

The man was livid. He was so mad his cheeks were red before he could speak again.

"Nigger, I'll kill ya dead if you er talk ta me like dat again."

It was the last complete sentence the man said for three days. Sam jumped on him just as he finished speaking, and he beat the man within an inch of his life.

And when the mob of white people jumped in to save the man's life, several of them were hurt trying to bring Sam down. But once the mob numbered more than ten, and fatigue began to overrun adrenaline,

Sam's time was up. They beat him so severely he was unrecognizable. The only reason they stopped pummeling him was because they wanted to "string him up" as a public example of why not to mess with "the good Christian white folks." MC wanted blood that day, but he wasn't ready to die.

Knowing that it would only be a matter of time before a mob of whites would come to terrorize the rest of the family for Sam's transgression, their father got his house in order and moved the family to Spartanburg where he had relatives. The move kept the family safe. Within a few years MC started his own family. He also served in World War II, being one of the first blacks to serve in the Marine Corps. The blatant discrimination in the Corps reaffirmed his avowal that something needed to be done.

When MC returned home from active duty, he confided in his quiet, easy-going son Rufus about his plans for the future. The Corps had taught him an advanced and extreme leveraging tool—murder. The way he saw it, it was practiced extensively by whites against blacks, but rarely the other way around, which he found unacceptable. He had killed whites in Europe who probably deserved it a lot less than most of the whites he encountered in America.

MC laid on Rufus's young ears his destiny, which was to add balance to the country by ridding it of a few bad Caucasians. He informed his son that when he was of age, he would join the military so that he could become efficient at killing. Once he was properly trained he would become a weapon against injustice. He stressed that quantity would never compare to quality.

Before MC checked out of the world, he made a few trips up to Greenville. Three white men went missing over the course of two months. After they found the shallow graves of the badly decomposed men, they set men to watch the town at night—the time of day each man went missing. During his fourth trip, these men caught MC sneaking about at night. When they recognized him and remembered that the three men murdered had participated in Sam's hanging, they quickly convicted Sam without a judge and hung him from the exact same tree as his brother.

Over the years, Samara's father had been living up to the high expectations of his father, but his time had run short. He wanted a son to carry on the legacy, but he didn't see it in them. Jesse, the older of the two brothers, was too busy chasing women and cared less about what his father wanted. It was Jesse first, and everyone else had to get in where they fit in. The younger brother, Marcus Calvin, was caught up in the streets. Rufus saw him as a follower.

Only Samara had the will to do her father's work. She was the only one intelligent and athletic enough to make it happen. She was able to take care of herself and others in extreme situations at a very young age. Rufus saw in her the potential to be far more powerful than him. Over the years he watched her become an effective leader who could make a great impact without the one-sided, very consequential life of an assassin that he had taken. But she was smart enough to use force when necessary.

Samara snapped out of her trance after Tonya bumped her.

"You're up next, girl," Tonya said. Samara simply nodded.

After the speaker introduced Samara she walked to the stage through a heavy roar of applause and cheers. She was one of the most popular and most reclusive students at the university. Some people suspected that

Tonya was her girlfriend, since Samara was on the basketball team, didn't have boyfriend, and rarely socialized with anyone else.

Samara stepped onto the stage and the applause continued for another twenty seconds. She smiled humbly and waited for the noise to subside. Once everyone stopped, a woman yelled, "That's my baby."

"I love you, too, Ma," Samara said and the audience laughed. "Good morning, everyone," Samara continued.

"Good morning," the audience sounded in unison.

"I know everyone wants to get the formalities over with and get to partying, because that's what most of y'all did for the last four years anyway." The audience laughed as the graduating students cheered. "Thank God for this ceremony. It's probably the first time this class has had 100 percent attendance and everyone sober or recuperating, trying to fight off a hangover." There was more laughter. "I won't hold y'all long.

"Today everyone leaves the school saying that you're an expert or have advanced knowledge in one field or another and that's beautiful. Through your hard work and perseverance, you've stepped up a notch on the economic chain. I mean, after you pay that first mortgage, also known as a student loan, back." Everyone laughed.

"But I hope you didn't attend Howard to get a decent to good paying job. I hope you didn't come to Howard for the parties and homecoming events. I hope you didn't come to Howard just to say you went to Howard.

"As a graduate of Howard you have a responsibility. Not to your parents or anyone else. You have a responsibility to the future. Inside these walls some of the greatest minds in African-American history were culti-

vated. And they inspired us to want more and to be
more. We as a whole have that responsibility to our future generations.

"We are not the Talented Tenth. We are a bunch of
young colored folk who made it. We are the each one,
teach one generation, and it's time we started putting
in work. With that being said, don't go and get your
white-collar job, Benz, and home in the suburbs and
forget that you graduated from Howard. Don't forget
that as a graduate of Howard you are charged with up-
lifting our people. Not just yourself, but our people.
We were a strong united front at one point, but now
we're segregated again.

"Don't think that it isn't necessary anymore because
the Civil Rights Movement is over. You would be fool-
ish to think that racism is dead. It is alive and well.
The new face of racism represents itself in the form of
socio-economic oppression, police profiling and bru-
tality, and in some of those fancy office jobs y'all are
going to get.

"The system, not just the criminal justice system,
but the system, if you know what I'm saying, is in
place to keep us in check. It is there to permanently
make us an underclass if we let it. Our fight is against
that system. And the way to weaken that system is to
get involved in the community. Go and talk to these
young brothers and sisters who are less fortunate and
in the streets. All they see is negativity in their neighborhood and on TV. And when we see them emulating
that foolishness, we shake our heads and turn our noses
up at them. And at the same time, they're offended by
us, because we think we're better than them. It's time
to put an end to all that foolishness, and it's time to
start with this class.

"There hasn't been a strong black leader not affiliated with the Civil Rights Movement for a long time, but here I am." Samara paused as she received a standing ovation and the applause became almost deafening. After more than a minute of applause, it slowly quieted. Samara, still standing at the podium, continued. "And here we are." The applause began again.

The ceremony continued. At the end of the graduation, all of the students headed out of the auditorium and met up with their family members outside. Everyone was trying to meet up with and congratulate Samara on her speech, and offer their support for her plans. Eventually she was able to meet up with her overly excited mother and brother, Marcus Calvin. Jesse was smiling, but he didn't care too much. He was too busy staring at all the exceptional young black women he hadn't had the chance of meeting and mating with.

"Baby, I'm so proud of you," Samara's mother Natalie said, and gave her a big hug. Marcus Calvin joined in. Jesse was conversing and laughing with another graduate who had come to congratulate Samara.

After the three separated, Samara asked, "Ma, have you seen Daddy?"

Natalie shook her head. "I haven't, baby. But I saw this young boy who looked like your father from around the time you were born." She paused. "We'll talk about that another day. Today is your day and we're going to enjoy it," Natalie said with a huge smile and another embrace. Samara managed a smile.

As they stood there Craig came over with balloons and flowers. He presented them to Samara. Natalie had a funny little smirk on her face.

"Uh hmm." She cleared her throat, alerting Samara that an introduction was necessary.

"Oh, this is New York," Samara said as she and Craig smiled. "I mean Craig."

"How are you doing, ma'am? Is it Mrs. Brown?" he asked to make sure he properly addressed her as he grabbed her hand for a gentle handshake. She nodded affirmatively. "Well, Mrs. Brown, it is a pleasure to meet you. I'm Craig, your future son-in-law."

Samara and her mother were astonished by the revelation. Marcus Calvin looked at him from head to toe and back to his face with a disapproving stare, basically sizing him up. Even with all the commotion and background noise, and despite being fully immersed in a conversation himself, Jesse turned to face Craig. As if it were rehearsed, Natalie and her children all said "What?!" in unison, with Samara's and Marcus Calvin's faces bordering on disgust.

Craig smiled.

"I'm just kidding. This is my buddy." He stood on her right side and grabbed her left shoulder, giving her light, buddy-like hug. "Y'all know we're both starting guards for the school. We're buddies like in the movie *Love and Basketball*."

"Whatever," Samara said, blushing a bit. Marcus Calvin finally recognized Craig.

"OK. You're Craig Miller. I saw you in the MEAC conference championship and the NCAA tournament. Hey, you got game for real. Are you going into the draft?"

"I appreciate that. I think I'm going to stick with Howard at least one more year. Hell, after that speech Samara just gave, I might stay for three more." They all laughed. "Please excuse me. Can I talk to Samara real quick and then I'll be out of y'all way so y'all can celebrate?" Craig asked, looking to Natalie for permission.

She nodded her head. He put the balloons and flowers in one hand, grabbed Samara's hand with the other, and led her to an area not crammed with people.

"I'm sorry we got off to a bad start the other day," Craig said.

"Don't worry about it. You caught me at a bad time."

"So we're cool now?" he asked, grinning from ear to ear.

"As long as you don't think your jumper is better than mine," Samara said, returning the smile.

"Whatever. We can play, for every shot made and the other person misses, that person loses some clothing."

"See, you're moving too fast," she said, turning to walk away from him.

Craig immediately grabbed her and turned her back around. "I was just playing, girl. It was in the movie. You can talk shit to me, but I can't say anything to you?"

She smiled. "You can, but tread lightly. I don't know you like that."

"That's what I wanted to ask you. Can we have dinner or something so we can get to know each other better?" Craig asked with a sincere, pleading look on his face.

"I don't think so," Samara answered.

Craig looked a little disappointed, but that faded quickly. "OK. How about this? We play a game of HORSE. You win, no date. If I win, date," Craig said with a smile.

Samara smiled against her will. She was just as attracted to Craig as she figured he was to her, but she looked at him as just another pretty-boy athlete with nothing on his mind except how many women he had, and a misplaced dream that sports was his only ticket to success, so she kept her distance. The more they interacted, though, the more her resistance dissipated.

She pondered the question a moment, and Craig continued his begging.

"I don't usually say this, but you're special, so PLEEEEASE!" Samara nodded, and Craig was overjoyed. "How about we do this tomorrow afternoon about one at the gym?" She nodded.

He hugged her, handed her the balloons and flowers, then left, anticipating the next's day's challenge, and savoring his small victory from today.

Chapter Five

The Audacity of Hope

Samara's rousing speech at graduation the day before did more for her than just gain her a few pats on the back and adoration from her peers. Many alumni and parents of graduates took note of Samara's pledge to be a leader and wanted to see what she had in store for the future. Knowing that her time would be limited and networking was a necessity to get her community center afloat, after the graduation ceremony was over, she passed out postcard-sized flyers to the people she thought were sincere and had the resources to help. She gave a brief description of her plans for the center and gave the time and place for a meeting the next day.

Samara had begun planning for her community center before she entered high school. She understood as a teenager the biggest problems with getting the center off the ground and running would have to do with money. Fortunately for her, her parents had started college funds for their children once they turned one, contributing one hundred dollars a month for each.

When Samara was a sophomore in high school, it became apparent that Jesse, a senior, had no plans of attending college, so his funds were reassigned to Samara's account. She was a senior in high school when her little brother Marcus Calvin had gotten arrested for carrying a concealed weapon while on probation for possession of drugs. He spent half of his tenth and most of what would have been his eleventh-grade year in a juvenile detention center. His funds were also reassigned to the only child who had a legitimate chance of going to college and being prosperous.

Samara had earned a full scholarship to Howard, so her college fund, compounded with interest and in excess of $60,000, was hers to do with as she pleased. On top of that, Rufus had set up a mutual fund account for Samara when she was just five years old that started with her father's total savings account and an equity line of credit from their Hillcrest single-family house in Southeast. The mutual fund cashed out at nearly six figures when she closed the account during her junior year of college. Taking an enormous gamble, she trusted her mother, Natalie, a certified public accountant and a highly regarded financial advisor, with her dreams and placed $120,000 into a high-risk, high-yield technology firm that returned her money four-fold within a year. She quickly extracted that money before the bubble burst.

She purchased an old abandoned building that used to house a boxing gym named the House of Champions, and slowly, but surely she began to renovate and extend it at the beginning of her senior year. The entire building was finished in April, about a month before she was set to graduate. The pride and joy she gained from seeing the renovation of the building, which she visited every day, was diminished only by the fact that her father might never see it.

The morning after graduation she had a grand presentation prepared. The attendees numbered about sixty with alumni, professors, business professionals, media and entertainment personalities, and working class people wanting to know what Samara was all about. To make the offer even more irresistible, she had breakfast catered from a black owned restaurant named Goins, which was located just down the street from the center.

Everyone arrived early or just on time. They were seated in the large two-story conference room near the front of the building. Samara took the floor with her best friend Tonya at her side.

"Good morning, everyone," Samara addressed the crowd.

"Good morning," they responded in unison.

"It's nice to see everybody here and on time. It's good to dispel the myth that our people are notoriously late, even though I know the free food prompted the punctual attendance." The audience got a light laugh to break the air and make the crowd feel comfortable.

"I personally hate long meetings because most of them can be summed up in about ten minutes, and I'm ready to eat. So this is how the presentation is going to go. I'll explain what programs will begin on opening day, what programs we hope to bring to the center in the coming months, what it will cost to make it happen, and the help we could use from you all as far as tax-deductible donations, and just as important, your time for mentoring and special programs. After I lay all that out for you, we'll take a quick tour and then we'll eat," Samara explained with a bit of excitement.

"First, let me introduce the staff. Tonya Wilson,"—

she pointed to her friend—"a fellow graduate and my best friend is the executive director. Keisha Jones, also a Howard alumna, is the program director. And we have a few other brothers and sisters working with us part-time and volunteering to get our children going in the right direction."

After that introduction Samara laid out her plans and goals for the center for the next five years. She took them on the tour and they ate. Everyone was thoroughly impressed. And although there were usually many questions when it came to people parting with their money, there was only one question that came from an alumnus who had made a small fortune in real estate investments.

"This is a pretty tough neighborhood. A lot of these children's parents don't give a damn. Do you think the center can be effective with their surroundings being as they are?" he asked.

"It has to be," Samara responded. "We've been failing our kids for a long time now. We've written off the ones in bad areas as if they can't be made into decent citizens. If we can instill some pride in them, show them what success looks like, maybe we can change their surroundings from extremely depressed to working class at least. We would do them they same disservice the city has if we don't try."

The morning had gone well for Samara. Her presentation netted the center more than $12,000 on the spot, and pledges for an additional $50,000. Along with the grants and the money she had left over after the renovations, the center's financial health was looking great.

It was nearly one in the afternoon by the time everyone had departed, and although she didn't want to admit it to herself, she was looking forward to her game against

Craig. If she lost the game she would be forced to go on a date with him, which was an idea she was warming to. Even if they weren't going to be a couple, Samara felt that there was some truth in her needing to get out and about a bit more, or "loosen up" as Tonya put it.

When Samara got to the gym at twelve forty-five PM, Craig was already there shooting around. Once he noticed Samara and looked at the time, he seemed a little embarrassed. They smiled at each other.

"That's right. Get all the practice in you can. You're gonna need it," Samara teased him. "What time did you get here?" He smiled even harder.

"Oh, I just got here five minutes ago," he responded.

"Whatever. I told you no once, but now I have to reaffirm it on this court."

"Look here, Maury—do you mind if I call you Maury?" Craig asked. She shook her head, indicating that she did not. "After I beat you in less than ten shots, I'll give you a chance at double or nothing."

"I hear you, but I'll have to advise you to check those fantasies at the door. In reality, after I win this thing, I'll be heading out the door without saying a word to you."

"You know you talk a lot of . . ." Craig's words fell off as Samara took off her warm-ups. Lust flashed across his face. Her beautiful face and sculpted body put him in a trance, not to mention his preference for light-skinned women.

I bet she doesn't even know that she's one of the finest women God has ever created, Craig thought while he stared at her with his mouth wide open. *She's smart, sexy, and can play ball. I'm going to have women on the side, but I have to do whatever it takes to get her in my life. I wasn't playing when I said she*

*was going to be my wife. I just had to play it off for the
family because they haven't gotten to know me yet.*

"Are you OK?" Samara asked, wondering what the
lurid stare was all about.

"Maury, you are so beautiful."

She blushed. "Thank you, but flattery won't get you
a date, only jump shots."

Chapter Six

The New Sheriff

The next day Samara showed up at the center about nine in the morning, and things had barely slowed down from the night before. There were less young people out there selling drugs, but they had just turned in a few hours ago and would be back out by noon. Of course there were still a lot of transients about. The heroin and crack addicts were moving back and forth looking for their next move like it was a job. The drunks were out, but less animated than the addicts.

That day represented the first day of the hard times for Samara. She had been in the community for nearly a year prepping the center without much interaction except for a couple young guys giving her unwanted attention. For the center to be a safe haven and place the youth could feel comfortable, there would have to be a serious cleanup, and it wasn't going to be easy.

She approached three young men who were enjoying their morning jays of marijuana right in front of the center.

"What's going on, fellas?" Samara asked them.

"What's up?" two of the teens, J-Rock and TD, responded.

The third, a neighborhood tough guy named Donté replied, "Hey, sexy, what's up wit' you?" Samara stared him down like a mother disappointed in her child.

"You know we're opening this community center today," she said.

"You work here?" Donté asked with a huge grin appearing on his face.

"Something like that. I'm the founder."

"Oh yeah. What you got up in there?" Donté asked.

"Basketball courts, a weight room, pool tables, ping-pong . . ."

"What, you running a jail in there?" Donté asked as his friends laughed. He passed the marijuana to TD. Ignoring him, Samara continued.

"Classrooms for job training, a computer training center and"—she took a long pause and stared Donté down from head to toe—"a boxing ring."

Mike, aka TD, and James, aka J-Rock, looked at Donté with surprise and a slight grin. It wasn't lost on them that Samara had basically offered him up.

"What's that's supposed to mean?" Donté asked with a serious frown on his face.

"You asked what was in there, and I told you."

"Who are you getting smart with?"

"Getting smart with? I'm the only one with some intelligence in this conversation."

"Who in da fuck do you think you're talking to?" Donté asked, receiving the jay from J-Rock. Samara sighed before continuing.

"Look, I would love to see y'all in there. I need y'all to help coach the youth basketball teams. I need y'all to come get some training so you can get a decent job and stop playing on borrowed time with the system. I need y'all to step up and start being leaders in the communities and stop being followers."

"Followers?" J-Rock and TD asked, looking at each other in disbelief that they were labeled as such.

"Whatchu mean followers?" Donté asked, tossing the marijuana aside and stepping in her face. He blew a thick cloud of smoke in her face. Samara began to grind her teeth and looked away to try to regain her composure. She turned back toward him and stared him dead in the eye.

"Starting today, smoking weed or any other illegal drug and drinking in front of, on the side of, or behind this center are strictly prohibited."

All three young men laughed their asses off.

"What you goin' do, call the police?" Donté asked, still half laughing.

"Not at all. We're going to make a little bet."

"A bet?"

"A simple bet. What's your name?"

"Tay," Donté said.

"I take it that's short for Donté."

He nodded in agreement.

"Well look here, Donté, here's the bet. We're gonna go in the gym and put on the gloves for one five-minute round. If I win, y'all participate in the activities I suggested and don't allow anyone, including yourselves, to smoke or drink around the building."

TD and J-Rock laughed. Donté was infuriated.

"Lady, I will beat the shit out of you," Donté said.

"I hear you talking, youngin'. Let's go put on the gloves and we can find out," Samara said flatly.

Craig walked up on the tail end of Samara and Donté's conversation, and interrupted.

"Let me holla at you right fast," Craig said to Donté.

Craig put his arm around Donté's shoulder and they walked down the street and away from Samara, TD, and J-Rock.

"Lady, do you really think you can whoop Tay?" J-Rock asked.

"I do. I hope we can come to an understanding without going through all of that, but if it's necessary, we'll find out." She looked down the street at Craig and Donté. There didn't seem to be any friction or fussing. Samara appreciated Craig trying to diffuse the situation, but she would have to inform him that she was able to take care of herself.

"Besides me and your boy's disagreement, what do y'all think about the things I said, liking helping these kids out and stuff?" Samara asked. "Let me help you get a job."

"What's your name?" J-Rock asked.

"Samara, but I go by Maury."

"Well, Maury, I'd be glad to be part of the center. Are you going to have boxing tournaments and training and stuff like that? You know, they really don't have that type of stuff in DC anymore."

"I know. We definitely can have some tournaments, and I can have some pros come through every now and then to give some encouraging words or possibly scout some talent." J-Rock began to bounce around with his fists up, throwing light punches into the wind while grinning from ear to ear. Craig and Donté finally returned.

"What? You tryin' to get my man to take your place or something?" Donté asked Samara playfully as he saw J-Rock warming up. Samara smiled.

"I don't want to fight you, brother. I just want a little respect, one way or the other."

"I didn't mean any disrespect. I just play a lot. Plus, you kind of embarrassed me a little bit in front of my men, so I had to get back."

"Well if it's any consolation to you, I told them if they didn't like what I had to say, they could see me right now."

Donté was caught between surprise and a grin. "For real?"

Samara smiled again. "I'm just kidding." They all got a light laugh from the exchange. After a few seconds, Samara came close to Donté and gave him a hug to the curious and envious eyes of Craig. Donté didn't want to release the embrace, and Samara had to pry herself from him.

"So are you going help me clean up this area?" Samara asked Donté. He nodded affirmatively. TD and J-Rock also agreed, even though she didn't direct the question to them. She went over and grabbed both of them so that all three of them were hugging each other. Donté joined in. Craig wanted to hug Samara, too, but couldn't see putting his free arm around the young men, so he stood where he was. Finally the three young men and Samara broke apart as if they were breaking from a huddle. They all entered the center and Samara showed them the things she had in store for the community.

Chapter Seven

Sassy-Ass Samara Brown

The biggest day of Samara's life had finally come to fruition. It was the community center's grand opening. Proudly displayed on the front of the building was the center's name—Future Leaders' Community Center. There was so much hype around the center's opening that people came from all over the city to attend.

It was a beautiful Saturday morning on Memorial Day weekend. The whole community, from the very young to the elderly came out to see about the new center that everyone was talking about. Of course the music, free food, drinks, and the Moon Bounce did their share in attracting the crowd, whose members included the city's mayor and the councilman for the ward. The police were there as well, just to make sure everyone stayed in line while the politicians and media mingled.

Samara and Tonya were in front of the center greeting everyone who came. After playing the politician and absorbing as much positive press and media spot-

light as possible, the mayor made his way around to
see Samara, who had made no special effort to see him.

"Ms. Brown, it's a pleasure to finally meet you. I've
heard such great things about you," Mayor Thomas
said, extending his hand. Samara accepted the handshake, nodded, and smiled. She wanted to reply, but if
Samara were to be honest, her comments probably
would have offended him, so she held her peace.

"I have a question for you, Ms. Brown," the mayor
said.

"What's that?"

"The way I understand it, you were the valedictorian
of your class with scholarships offered for advanced
degrees, a prospect for the WNBA draft, and a few
white-collar job offers, but you rejected them all and
put in your own money to start this center. Is that
true?"

"It is."

"You must really be committed, huh?"

"I am."

"And there's no way I can get you to come work for
Human Services either, right?"

"Not even if you made me the director and paid me
the equivalent of your salary."

The mayor smiled and shook his head. "Yeah, well
you're better than me."

Samara smiled. "There's no question about that."

The mayor's smile faded and there was a slight moment of tension. From a distance of about twenty feet
away a reporter who was talking with the councilman
noticed the mayor's smile evaporate quickly and saw a
front-page story forming in its absence.

"Excuse me," the reporter said, abandoning the
councilman while he was still speaking. She made a

beeline for Samara and the mayor. The councilman, wondering what was more important than what he had to say, followed her.

After a small crowd had formed around Samara and the mayor, he looked around at the people and laughed off Samara's comment.

"You're outspoken too. I like you already," the mayor said to Samara, and she smiled again. The mayor pulled her close and whispered in her ear. "At some point, you're going to need public funds, so it would behoove you to keep me on your side and subdue the sassiness."

"At some point, you're going to have to pretend that you actually care about the youth in this city, and you are going to need my help," Samara whispered back. "So it would behoove you not to get on my nerves or I'll ban you from the center." Samara moved back and greeted the mayor with a huge smile. His face was very tight at first, but he managed to smile as well.

"You drive a hard bargain, but it's a deal," the mayor said, playing off their whispered conversation as a negotiation, when it was actually an ultimatum.

"Thank you, sir." Samara played along with the mayor, although the conversation had been nothing short of a rebuke. She figured that response would allow him to save face and dissipate some of his anger at her words. "Would you like to take a tour of the facility, Mr. Mayor?" Samara asked in a pleasant tone. It was at that moment that his anger seemed to disappear entirely.

"Certainly," he said. Samara led him into the building. As he followed her, he couldn't help but watch her hips and the way her not-so-tight or revealing dress clung to her body like lingerie. In his eyes Samara had it all—a body, brains, and a passion for what she believed in. He would gladly trade in his wife for her, or at least have her on the side like so many other young city government workers he had befriended.

After Samara led the mayor, councilman, and the media on a tour of the facility, all seemed quite impressed. As they exited, they ran into a situation just outside the building. Three uniformed police officers were putting the press on Donté and J-Rock. Samara immediately headed to where the confrontation was taking place. Following her were the mayor, the councilman, and the media.

Arriving on the scene first, Samara stood silently and observed. As two of the officers frisked the young men for illegal substances or weapons, a third female officer named Officer Presto took a step toward Samara. Samara's disgust was obvious from the frown on her face.

"Is there a problem?" the female officer asked Samara.

"Is there a problem?" Samara repeated, obviously surprised at the officer's aggressiveness. The mayor, councilman, and journalist entered the scene along with a small crowd. "Yes, there's a problem. I thought it was this situation where two young men are being harassed at a peaceful event. But now I see that it's you."

All three officers, realizing they had the attention of two of the most important politicians representing the area they were assigned to watch over, suddenly took heed of their words and actions. They finished searching the young men and allowed them to leave, but J-Rock and Donté stayed behind to watch the scene unfold.

Samara turned to the trio of the mayor, councilman, and reporter.

"See, this is the kind of foolishness that we have to

contend with," she said. "These young men haven't committed a single crime, but they are treated like criminals even at this function where everyone is laughing and playing and having fun. James and Donté work for the center and have helped to make this event a success, and you have these incompetent officers harassing them without cause."

All three officers took exception to being called incompetent, but Officer Presto became livid.

"Who in the hell are you calling incompetent?" Officer Presto asked.

"Or ignorant," Samara continued. "Whichever is preferable."

The mayor stepped in, attempting to diffuse the situation. "Hold on now," he said. "Y'all young ladies calm down. Ms. Brown, I understand your frustration, but the name calling isn't necessary." Samara held her peace. "I know Ms. Brown was a little out of line, but she does have a valid concern," the mayor said, effectively straddling the fence. He needed the police on his side, but he knew he had to address the obvious racial profiling that had happened right in front of his face since the nosey reporter was at his side.

The officers seemed a little hesitant. One of the two male officers spoke up.

"Sir, we thought we witnessed marijuana being rolled by these two men and the other young men who left the scene."

"Ain't nobody rolling no damn marijuana," J-Rock interjected. "We were over here chillin' when they walked over and started searching us. We weren't doing anything except standing over here talking."

"And the reason that the other people who were with us walked off is because these same officers harass us every day," Donté continued. "They search us without cause. They verbally and physically abuse us. It's just like being locked up in your own community. You see what I'm sayin'? They dictate to us which of our rights they're going to respect."

A roar of cheers and applause came from the crowd that had formed. Samara looked at the mayor for an explanation. The mayor looked back at Samara, then the reporter, who had a micro-recorder and a pad in one hand and a pen in the other, feverishly taking notes while the machine recorded every word.

The councilman, seeing that the mayor was hesitant and that he would have the opportunity to steal some of the spotlight, interjected.

"I can't believe in this day and age we still have problems with police violating the rights of the citizens they are here to protect. This behavior is unacceptable and will not be tolerated in my ward."

"And not in my city," the mayor continued. "I think we have to reverse the trend of seeing all young black males as criminals or potential criminals. I think this center will go a long way in helping bridge the gap between this community and the police. I'm going to sponsor a civilian oversight board in every ward to monitor complaints against the police abusing their powers. I think Ms. Brown with her commitment to the community would be an excellent choice to head up the committee for this ward."

The entire audience clapped and cheered except for the three police officers involved and the other officers in the crowd.

Officer Presto shook her head, leaned in close to Samara, and whispered, "This isn't over."

"Not at all. I have a boxing ring in the center. Come and see me on your day off," Samara replied.

Chapter Eight

The Long Kiss Goodnight

The opening of the center had been a success. All of Samara's and Tonya's hard work had paid off. To celebrate, Tonya insisted that they go out and enjoy themselves. Samara refused at first, but eventually Tonya won her over.

Just as Samara pulled up her pants, there was a knock at the door. Samara, wearing only her tight fitting dress pants and a bra, walked over to the door. She looked through the peephole and was greeted by Tonya's big, beautiful smile and another person standing behind her.

"Open the door, girl," Tonya said from the other side. Samara opened the door as Tonya and Keisha, one of their girlfriends and a staff member at the center, entered.

"Maury, what's taking you so long?"

"I was trying to decide whether I was going with y'all."

"Girl, I've already decided that for you. All you have to do is decide what you're going to wear. And if you need help with that . . ."

"Child, please. I should have helped you to dress," Samara retorted.

"What?" Tonya inquired as she spun in a circle with her very tight and revealing dress clinging to her body. "You don't like my outfit?"

"Sure, if that's what you're going to sleep in." Keisha laughed. "I know for the amount of money you paid for that outfit, they could have given you more material than that. You know they don't allow you to wear negligees in the club."

"Whatever, grandma. I look good."

"There's no question about that. Tonya, you're very pretty and sexy, but do you need all the extra attention that outfit brings?"

"I do. I usually get plenty of attention, but since I'm bringing your pretty and sexy, but socially inept ass, I might have some competition. Even though you shoot them all down, men are always hawking you. Besides, I'm classy 350 days out of the year. Therefore, I reserve the right to dress however I please once a month and on certain holidays." All three of the women laughed.

"Girl, you're crazy," Samara said.

"I know. We work hard. We need to have some fun."

"Speaking of fun," Keisha interjected, "who is that fine-ass brother that keeps coming by the center looking for you, Maury?"

"Who, Craig?" Tonya responded for her. "You still ain't gave him none yet?"

"Tonya?" Samara asked with her mouth wide open in embarrassment.

"Tonya what?"

"You know I'm not like that."

"I know. That's why I'm trying to help you out. You need some stress relief and here's the prescription—get some."

"See, that's your problem now. You keep giving these men who ain't worth the time of day your precious time and your body."

"The thing is I like boys, not toys. I like body heat, not batteries. I'll give a man my time if he makes it worth it," Tonya said, placing her hands on her hips.

"See, that's your problem now. You need Jesus in your life."

"I got Jesus in my life, but until I get another good man, I'll pick and choose." The three women laughed at Tonya's proclamation.

About forty-five minutes later they arrived at the H20 club on the waterfront in the Southwest section of the city. The three waited in the line to be thoroughly searched and pay the admission fee. There were plenty of people in the club and plenty more on the outside waiting to get in.

Samara, Tonya, and Keisha were getting plenty of attention before they even stepped foot inside the club. Police officers working security and the bouncers at the door were all trying their luck at talking with the young ladies. Tonya flirted with everyone that flirted with her. Keisha was a bit more reclusive. Samara wasn't saying much of anything. She just politely smiled and kept it moving.

They entered the club and headed for the bar. Before they could get comfortable men were in their ears offering drinks. Tonya and Keisha soaked up the attention, but Samara wanted to hide.

Samara wasn't comfortable at all. There were too many people too close to her. She also didn't like the fact that she was completely unarmed. She didn't even have a knife in an environment that could be volatile inside or out. On top of that, she had a very drunk, alcohol-smelling man all in her face. Samara wasn't sure she would qualify the night as fun up to that point.

As the man was trying hard to get Samara's name out of her, another one came to her other side and whispered in her ear.

"I won the game. Now how's about that date?"

Samara turned around to a smiling Craig. She couldn't help but return his smile. He patiently waited for her answer.

Just as she nodded in agreement, the boozer on her right had a few words for Craig.

"Hold on, slim. Why is you . . . all up . . . in my girl's ear?"

"Let's go before I have to knock this nigga out," Craig said to Samara.

Samara got up and turned to leave with Craig. The man grabbed her arm. Before he could pull her back toward him, Samara elbowed the man in the nose with same arm he grabbed. It sent him sprawling to the floor. His head hit the floor hard, knocking him unconscious as blood spewed from his nose.

Samara walked a few feet over to where Tonya was having a lively conversation with a man with a lot of expensive clothing and jewelry. When Tonya saw Samara and Craig, she smiled. Samara moved close to Tonya's ear so that she could be heard over the loud music being played.

"We're going on a date."

"Get some," Tonya responded, and Samara laughed.

They made their way to Craig's Mercedes. He went to the passenger side, opened the door, and helped her in. Samara reached across the console and opened the driver's side door before Craig could get to it. He sat down and smiled at her and she blushed. They pulled off.

"Craig?"

"Yeah."

"Whose car is this?"

"Mine. Why do you ask?"

"How did you get it?"

Stopped at a red light, he turned to look at her. "What are you getting at, Samara?"

"This car costs a lot of money. If someone gave you this car as a gift for attending or playing for Howard, you could get kicked out of school."

A huge grin filled with relief crossed his face.

"It was a gift from my parents. My father heads up this brokerage firm and he's loaded. It was a high school graduation gift for graduating with honors and getting a full scholarship. To be truthful, though, I think they bought it with the money I wasn't going to need for school since I got the scholarship."

They enjoyed a light laugh. About a half hour later they arrived at Morton's Steakhouse, an upscale restaurant on Connecticut Avenue in Northwest. After having the valet take the car, they entered the restaurant. As Samara led and Craig followed, he was transfixed by the way her jeans fit, and that sexy and commanding walk of hers.

"Uhm, uhm, uhm," Craig said to himself in a very low tone while caught up in Samara's sex appeal.

Samara turned to him. "The food smells that good, huh?" she asked, smiling.

Surprised that she had heard him, and realizing that she knew his comments were about her, he decided not to answer.

They had a beautiful dinner filled with great food and good conversation. Samara didn't want to admit it, but she was falling for Craig. The more they got to know each other, the more she realized that he was more than just a pretty-boy basketball player. He was sweet and a natural at charming the ladies. Surprisingly, he was intelligent, too. Although, there was something about him that wasn't quite right, but Samara couldn't put her finger on it yet.

They pulled up at Samara's house, which she had been renting since she started college. She had considered having him drop her off elsewhere, but after thinking about it, she decided it really wasn't that big of a concern. If he had ever showed up uninvited or on the wrong terms, she had more than a few deterrents stashed in her house.

"Do you need me to see you in?" he asked.

"Yeah, you can watch from the car."

"Well can I get a good night kiss?"

"I have to get out in order to bend over."

Craig was visibly shocked. He couldn't believe that she had offered him her ass to kiss.

"Samara, why are you so cold, girl? We're both adults. I think we're feeling each other. I didn't ask to have sex with you. All I asked for was one little kiss. If you don't like it, I will never ask again."

Samara considered his proposal. She wanted to kiss him, but didn't want to let down her guard. Even though she was mentally and physically tough, she was still a woman who hadn't had the affection of a man in a long time. She was very attracted to Craig, which in turn made her very vulnerable. She couldn't see herself as one of his groupies.

"One kiss," she agreed.

He leaned in. She leaned away. He paused. He moved in slower, grabbing her shoulder. Their lips met, then their tongues. They shared a long, passionate kiss as he caressed the back of her head with his right hand and slipped his left hand over her right breast. He felt her hard nipple as he worked her over with his hands just as much as with his lips. They moved closer. She put her hand on his man and found that he was very much turned on as well. He attempted to feel between her legs and it ended instantly. She regained focus and exited the car immediately.

Before she closed the door, she turned to him and said, "I hope you enjoyed the kiss. It will be the last."

"Whatever. You sure you don't want me to see you in?"

"Good night, Craig," Samara said as she slammed the door and headed up the stairs.

He watched her walk up the stairs and wondered why he wasn't walking with her. He could not wait to have her. How could she do him like that? Leave him in the car with his Johnson fully erect and throbbing. He figured that when she finally gave in, he would make her pay for tonight.

He rolled down the window and said, "Good night, baby."

She smiled and slammed her front door.

Uhm, uhm, uhm. Wait until I get a hold of you, Ms. Brown, Craig thought. *You'll definitely be my main girl. I might even cut a few of them back for you. I gotta get you in my life.*

Samara was in her bedroom looking at Craig through the scope of her .22-caliber rifle with her nipples still erect and her underwear soaked. She didn't plan on shooting him. She just wanted to see the kind of impression she had left on him, because he had left a hell of an impression on her. After a moment he pulled off. That night she wanted the real thing, but refused to sacrifice her dignity for it, so she had to settle for the Energizer bunny and battery operated satisfaction.

Chapter Nine

Too Much Smoke

Early the next morning Samara rose and prepared herself for the day. She had really enjoyed her night out with Craig. She enjoyed it so much it was all she could think about that morning. As she ate a healthy bowl of oatmeal, she turned on the television.

Samara was truly disappointed by what the news had to offer. The highlights of the news included nothing but violence. There was a homicide here and multiple shooting victims there. All of the victims were black, under forty years old, and male. All of the joy she felt when she awoke dissipated in an instant. She realized that her center was only the beginning in turning the tide of negativity in the city.

About an hour later she was at the center preparing to open for the day. She was met by Donté, who seemed agitated. They entered the center together, and Donté locked the door behind them.

"What's wrong?" Samara asked, sensing Donté's anxiety. He paused for a moment to get himself together.

"We've had this on again, off again beef with this

crew further up the avenue. A few days ago this nigga named Smoke"—Samara raised her eyebrows, alerting him that the use of "nigga" was unacceptable in her presence—"my bad. A few days ago this dude named Smoke got out of jail after doing a five-year bid with the feds. About a year ago, some people from our crew killed his little brother on their block. We've been going back and forth since then, but Smoke is like the ringleader for their crew. He's quick to shoot and don't really have any cut cards about when and where he does it."

Samara nodded. "So this guy is going to be a problem."

"Believe me, he's going to be much more than a problem. He's got balls, too. He came through last night and had a few words for us. He drove through our neighborhood solo and said, 'Y'all bitch-ass niggas killed my little brother, so now that I'm back y'all already know what it is. I'ma punish all y'all.' A couple of people went to their stash and got the hammers to let loose, but he was out of range when they started shooting."

"So you think they'll be back and soon, huh?"

"No doubt. I'm telling you all this because he goes hard and his boys will follow his lead. He's going to come through, and since I'm sure his boys told him that we hang in here a lot, they might bring the beef inside this center."

Samara's facial expression was one of pure amazement.

"What! Oh, naw. We can't have that."

"I know," Donté agreed. "I was just letting you know so that you can keep your head up and to let you know that we're going to be strapped from now on."

"I really admire your intentions on protecting yourself, your friends, and the center, but having a bunch of y'all in here toting guns isn't the answer. In fact, it would only make things worse. No guns."

Donté's face contorted in confusion.

"Ms. Brown, are you trying to tell me that you ain't strapped right now?" Samara looked both worried and embarrassed. "It's just between us," Donté said.

Slightly relieved, Samara asked, "How did you find out about that?"

"Let's say I was taught to be aware of my surroundings. It's kept me out of jail and above ground." It was a trait she wished her brother would learn. Samara nodded, acknowledging that she understood. She understood that he was very attentive, or else she was slipping. In any case, she respected his intelligence. With a little guidance she may have found herself an apprentice.

"Look, Ms. Brown, Smoke coming home is serious, especially since he knows we were responsible for killing his brother. We know for sure he has a couple of bodies. He's supposed to be in for life right now, but he got the major charges thrown out when the police jacked up the evidence. Ain't none of us no suckers or anything like that, but this nigga . . . I mean this dude is on another level. He has no respect for anybody or anything. When he was twelve, he brought a gun into junior high school and shot three people from a gang they were beefing with. It's not going to be pretty."

Samara was beginning to understand the severity of the situation. The thought that Smoke or any of his friends would bring the beef into the center was unacceptable. The fact they were threatening to put innocent children in harm's way was bad enough. If something so dear to Samara was violated by foolishness, it would come with a severe price for the perpetrators.

"I understand, but no guns in the center," Samara re-iterated. Donté nodded reluctantly. "I know the situation is bad, but this is the first time you've been on time for work," Samara said, smiling, and they both enjoyed a laugh.

About five minutes later Tonya showed up for work. Samara quickly informed her of the situation in its entirety. As each member of her staff arrived, she informed them of the basics, which was that there was a neighborhood beef going on, and they needed to be careful and pay attention.

Even though everyone was on edge, the day went by without any complications. Everyone had a good day at the center. It was at a quarter to nine, just fifteen minutes before closing, before all of that changed.

Just outside the center gunshots rang out. Most of the people in the center crouched low and looked nervous. Samara got low and kept her hand in her purse. She usually kept her weapon in a safe place in her office, but after Donté's warning earlier in the day, she put her piece in her purse and kept her purse at her side.

When the loud percussions nullified all sound before it, it made Samara's heart drop to know that someone was in a bad situation. For a few seconds she felt helpless as she knew that that sound often forced change in people's lives, and the result was never positive. It hurt her more to know that what happened on the other side of the door was beyond her control.

"Everyone stay down," Samara yelled.

The initial firing ceased. A few seconds later there was return fire. Samara cautiously made her way to the door.

"Maury," Tonya yelled to her friend. She knew that Samara was going outside, but she was hoping she could get her to wait. Samara only briefly glanced at her friend before proceeding out the door.

Samara walked out the door with her hand in her purse, and the safety off. She took in the entire scene within seconds. Three people lay on the ground, obviously suffering from gunshot wounds. Two young men were running away from the scene with guns in their hands. Samara figured they may have been the assailants, but most likely they were a few of the young men from the neighborhood who had returned fire. She went back to check on the injured. She recognized all three, but she was especially hurt to see J-Rock and TD among the injured. J-Rock was the only person both conscious and breathing. Samara ran over and kneeled beside him.

"Maury," J-Rock said, grimacing in pain.

"Yes?"

"I was just taking a smoke break," he said, followed by a weak laugh. Sirens blared in the distance, constantly getting louder. She smiled.

"This is another example of why smoking is bad for your health," she said. J-Rock smiled, unable to laugh because of his injuries.

"Where are you hit?" Samara asked.

"One in the leg and one in my stomach."

"This is what I need for you to do. Stay calm and try not to talk much, but if you get drowsy, try to talk forever if you have to. You're going to be fine." She slowly lifted his blood soaked shirt and saw the huge hole in his abdomen. Now she wasn't sure about her assurances to J-Rock. The blood flowed freely. She removed her T-shirt, exposing her tank top and bra. Samara folded the shirt into a small square and applied pressure to the wound.

The police arrived and took over the scene. They began to interview everyone. EMTs and firefighters arrived a moment or two later. They ushered all the young men that were shot to the Washington Hospital Center about a quarter of a mile away.

Samara wanted to check on the young men who had been attacked, but she knew it would be hours before their status could be determined, unless someone died. Given the brazen nature of Smoke as described by Donté, she figured he would not be hard to find. She needed to have a few words with him.

She sat in her car for about twenty minutes before leaving. Her hesitation was not caused by fear of what might happen to her when she rolled into their neighborhood, but fear of what she might do to them. Samara was too upset and emotional to make any important decisions. Her father had warned her that taking action under those emotions often led to mistakes. The mistakes she had envisioned would have her rotting in jail or dying that night. She took the time to regain her composure.

Tonya walked up to the passenger side door and opened it. Samara was so deep in thought that she hadn't noticed Tonya until she was getting in. Tonya was not surprised to find Samara putting her gun away as she sat down. The second Tonya opened the door Samara's gun was drawn on her, but as soon as she realized that the person entering the car was her friend, she put it away.

"Maury," Tonya called out to her friend, who stared blankly out the windshield. Samara slowly turned her attention to her friend. "Where you going?"

"To the hospital," Samara said blandly.

"Good, then I'll ride with you."

"Naw, I'll meet you there."

"Samara, who do you think you're playing with? I

know you better than you know yourself. You don't think I know where you're going?"

"Well, if you know me, then you know why I can't get you involved."

"I've been involved since we were six years old and in the first grade, when the little fat girl from the fourth grade kept bullying everyone, especially me, and you put an end to that as soon as you got to the school. Or the time those girls from around the way tried to jump me. Or the time one of my boyfriends went upside my head and you handled that. I got involved the day we became friends."

"Tonya, I love you. I can't put you in harm's way."

"Samara, I love you. I can't allow you to put yourself in harm's way."

When Samara figured she would not be able to persuade Tonya to get out of the car, she started it up and headed to the hospital. They were there for about an hour with a host of police and people from the community waiting on the status of J-Rock and TD. The third victim, Tim, had been pronounced dead on arrival.

"Where are you going?" Tonya asked Samara when she suddenly got up from her seat beside Tonya.

"To the ladies' room, if that's all right with you, Mommy," Samara said with blatant sarcasm. Tonya eyed her suspiciously before returning her gaze to the TV in the emergency room's waiting area.

Samara went straight out the front door, hopped in her car, and headed straight up Georgia Avenue. She made a right on Kennedy Street and pulled up to a corner across the street from a group of young men. In the midst of the group a dark-skinned man in his mid-twenties held court. He sounded like a storefront preacher, and he held his audience captive.

Samara rolled down her window.

"Smoke," she called across the street.

He frowned, squinted his eyes, and bobbed his head from left to right.

"Who is that?" he asked.

"Come and see," she responded.

"Get outta the car."

She started up the car, preparing to leave, and he immediately walked over to her.

"Damn, girl, you cute as shit. Where do I know you from?"

"You don't. Let me tell you what you need to know. Whatever little beef you have with the guys down the street, you need to keep away from the center."

"Who da fuck is you? You better mind your motherfuckin' business. Bitch, I will kill you."

"OK, let it happen again," Samara said, daring him.

He attempted to open the door, but she quickly pulled off. He lifted his shirt, extracted a 9 mm Beretta, and opened fire.

Samara sped away from the scene. Her anger was kindled.

Chapter Ten

Brazen

Samara awoke at about five-thirty in the morning after tossing and turning all night. Her life had changed the night before, and she was trying to figure out the best way to handle it.

The night before an event transpired that her father had warned her about. Rufus had told Samara that the life he taught her would conflict with the things she wanted to accomplish and the things she wanted to believe in.

He explained to her, "With any mission, there will be complications. There are two things that can make or break it. First, emotions and action will get you arrested or killed. Second, and more importantly, you are very good at reasoning and persuading. But not everyone is intelligent enough to listen to reason. They only understand their way, and violence as an act of persuasion. If that person is black, and you have to defend yourself or eliminate a threat, you can't let it break you."

Prophetically his words rang true. Smoke, as far as
Samara was concerned, was already dead. She spent
the night trying to figure out a way to save his life. He
had committed an unforgivable sin. He failed to kill
her, and she had learned early on that if someone tried
to take her out and failed, that someone and their ac-
complices were not to get a second chance.

Samara was at a crossroads. Her anger and the training her father gave her would not allow the young man
to live. The things her mother had taught her told her
there had to be another way. Since the young man had
already been sentenced to death, she was trying to stay
the execution.

While Samara was deep in thought, the phone rang.

"Hello."

"Samara, if you ever pull a move like that again, I'm
gonna have to see you in that boxing ring," the caller
said.

Samara sighed. "I'm sorry, Tonya. I could not put you
in harm's way."

"Maury, we're like sisters. I'm with you no matter
what happens. If it's too dangerous for me, then maybe
it's too dangerous for you, too. If you want me to be with
you through thick and thin, then it's going to be always
or never."

There was a long pause in the conversation.

"OK."

"OK what?" Tonya asked.

"If we're together and it's too dangerous to take you,
I won't go either."

Tonya was relieved. "So where did you go last night?"
she asked.

"Tonya?"

"I'm sorry. I'll talk to you when I see you."

Samara did not like to discuss anything of importance over the phone. Simply calling Tonya's name had reminded Tonya of that.

"Are J-Rock and the other guy OK?" Samara asked.

"Yes. They're going to be all right."

"Good. I'll see you at the center in a little while."

"OK."

It was midday and the center was bustling. There was a heavy concentration of police all around the center and the surrounding neighborhood. They were on foot, on bikes, and constantly riding around the neighborhood in their squad cars.

They harassed everyone. People were getting searched with no probable cause whatsoever. There were roadblocks where they randomly pulled over cars and checked the driver's credentials. They had even searched a young man they followed into the center. Samara had words with them and they didn't search anyone else, but with their boldness she could not keep her gun on her person as she had planned to do.

As Samara was helping one of the kids with an arts and crafts project, Donté pulled her to the side.

"What's up, Donté?"

"Nothing much. I was just wondering if you were carrying your pocketbook around today." They both laughed.

"I think we should limit access to the center," Donté continued.

"Huh?"

"I'm just saying, you know how at the end of the day we have someone on the door to lock it as people leave and to prevent anyone else from coming in?" Samara nodded. "I think we should do it all day until you can get a buzzer entry system."

"I understand and I agree. Between me and you, I went up there to have a few words with Smoke last night." Donté looked surprised. "He's hotheaded like you said. I think he is stupid enough to bring that bull-shit into the center. We need to figure out how we're going to work that out. I'll talk to Tonya about it and get back with you." Donté nodded and headed back over to the basketball court.

It was almost four in the afternoon when Samara caught up with Tonya. They went over the game plan for securing the building. They were in the process of calling a staff meeting and informing everybody of the new rules regarding access to the building when the door opened.

The major police shift changes were well defined in the city. A good portion of the patrol officers' shift changes were at eight AM, four PM, and midnight. Not all police were taken from the streets during those times, but their presence declined significantly.

Using a bit of strategy and boldness Samara did not think he was capable of, Smoke and three masked ac-complices entered the center and extracted guns. Smoke's face was covered with a bandana and a base-ball cap, but his dreads and what Samara saw in his eyes gave him away.

Samara was in trouble. She had too many people to get out of harm's way, and no gun to protect them or herself. She didn't have time to get her gun. There were kids as young as three running around playing before the quartet came into the center and assumed control.

Samara was about thirty feet from the door where the young men stood with their guns drawn. People began to scatter everywhere. There were many women and children screaming and young adults and men running for their lives. The staff workers attempted to move the small children out of the way.

"There are children in here," Tonya yelled at the assailants.

"Fuck 'em," Smoke yelled back and began to open fire. The sound was deafening inside the center. One of the kids began to run as the gunshots rang out. Samara had to run and tackle the little girl to keep her out of the line of fire. The child was hysterical. The shooting paused for a second. Samara grabbed the child and began to run with her in her arms to safety behind a wall.

Behind the wall Samara extracted a knife she was carrying. She got a good line of sight on Smoke and steadied her aim. She wanted to put the blade between his eyes, but with so much commotion and such a small target, she decided to pick the largest visible area—his torso. She was hoping to hit him in the heart.

Samara had acquired her target. Just as she prepared to throw, there was return fire from the other side of the center. She threw the knife, but the bullets traveling in the direction of Smoke and his boys caused them to retreat, altering her target by less than a foot. The knife barely missed Smoke. The return fire had knocked down two of the accomplices.

Samara looked over and saw Donté and TD firing at the young men. Smoke was the first one out the door. As his buddy followed him through the door he was hit in the back twice, causing him to collapse outside the door. Donté and TD ran toward the door. Each of the young men by the door received a single shot to the head.

Running out the door, they saw Smoke get in a car with its engine idling, and speed off. Donté and TD sent their last couple of shells at the vehicle. Afterward they ran away from the scene.

Inside the center Samara checked out the damage. A seven-year-old boy named Trey was shot in the leg. Five young black men associated with Donté's crew were hit. By the looks of it, two of them were dead. The other two were in bad shape, along with one of the staff members. Marcus was unscathed.

The one thing Samara was sure of was that Smoke had tried to kill her twice. He would not get a third shot. After she saw his indifference to children, separating his soul from his body would be easy. The roadblock of killing another young black male had been lifted. She had no problem killing monsters, and she could see that Smoke was beyond rehabilitation. She wondered whether he would be so tough where she was sending him. Hell hath no fury like Samara Brown.

Chapter Eleven

Ride and Die

Soon after the shootout took place in the center, Samara wanted to take off after Smoke and gun him down, but her father had taught her better. With her emotions running so high, her actions would have landed her ten years or better in the federal penal system. She knew what she had to do. It was just a matter of figuring out the best way to do it.

If Samara had left the center after such an incident, any excuse for leaving before emergency services showed up would have sounded suspect. If a fourth young man wound up dead from the same crew during the time that Samara had no alibi, then she went to jail for murder. She had to be patient.

Paramedics and police officers were on the scene within minutes. After removing the injured, the medics left. Left on the scene were dozens of police officers, detectives, and a couple of corpses. Just on the other side of the building countless reporters and some politicians tried to gather as much information as possible.

The officers interviewed everyone, and the stories

stayed pretty consistent. Everyone had hidden or was cringing on the floor as soon as the shots went off, so they didn't get a chance to see Donté and TD finish off the young men. And they had stashed their guns and were back in the building before the police had showed up.

Late in the evening when the police had finally interviewed everyone and reconstructed the crime scene to their liking, Samara closed the center. The police informed her that the center would have to remain closed for at least twenty-four hours.

Early the next morning Samara and Tonya met at the center. Donté joined them. The center was closed to all children and activities, but not to the staff. Samara had already placed an order with a contractor for the installation of a buzzer entry system.

Inside her office, which was not part of the crime scene, Donté approached Samara.

"Ms. Brown," Donté said. Samara looked up. "Can I go with you?"

"What! What are you talking about? Can we go to the hospital?"

Donté looked Samara squarely in the eyes. "Can I go with you?" He reiterated very slowly.

Samara was very confused. She looked at the young man and wondered if he could see her thoughts. Did he know that she had the capacity to kill? Had he figured out that her next move was to eliminate the threat? Most importantly, who was this kid?

She stared at the young man. He nodded in agreement. She shook her head. He nodded even harder.

"No."

"Why?" he asked.

"Because I said so."

He dismissed her by waving his hand. "You act just like my brother."

"What brother?"

"My brother Mike."

"Where is he?"

"In the feds."

"How long has he been in, and how much more time does he have?"

"He's been in three years. He should be coming home real soon."

"What's he in for?"

"I'll let him tell you."

"Is he the one who taught you to be so perceptive?" Samara asked, and Donté nodded. Samara leaned in close. "Is that the first time you've killed someone?" she whispered. He shook his head, indicating that it was not.

"And I know you have before, too," he said. "And I know that you're not going to let this ride. I also know that Smoke is a dead man. I just want to watch your back."

She backed away with a huge look of surprise and smiled.

"You know a little too much. I might have to take you out." They both laughed.

"Better we go together than I or you go alone and something happens to one of us," Donté said.

Although he had a valid point, Samara would have none of it.

"Donté, you're special. I can't ruin your life by putting you in the middle of this."

"I'm already in the middle of it."

She looked at Donté very sternly. "If you say I remind you of your brother, then you should know that my answer was final."

He was visually disappointed, but nodded in agreement.

"When will I meet your brother?" she asked.

"Soon, I hope. I've been telling him about you for weeks. He's very impressed. He said he's going to write you." Samara smiled.

It was a little past nine that night when Samara finally caught up with Smoke. She had been in and around the neighborhood for the past two hours looking for her man. At one point she was disguised as an elderly woman, complete with a salt and pepper colored wig and makeup to simulate a woman in her early seventies. Samara thoroughly cased the neighborhood.

Smoke and an associate got out of a car and went to the neighborhood carryout. Samara spotted them and had to quickly formulate a plan. She only wanted to rid the world of Smoke, so she would have to find a way to separate the two and the target from existence.

The young men returned to the car with the smell of chicken and mumbo sauce. Smoke sat in the driver's seat and his man in the passenger's seat. Just after Smoke turned the ignition, and a second before the radio came back on, the very loud click-clack of a shell being loaded into the chamber caught both men by surprise.

Plap! Plap! She smashed both men across the head with the gun. Both of them attempted to bolt from the vehicle. The passenger escaped. Samara grabbed Smoke by the collar and placed the gun to his head. He sat back in the seat and looked in the rearview mirror. All he saw was someone wearing a ski mask.

Disguising her voice to sound like a man, she said, "Close the doors, lock them, and drive." When their eyes met in the rearview mirror again, she saw fear in his. Smoke knew that this might very well be his last ride. He had to think fast. His hesitation made him the recipient of a second blow across the head with the silenced barrel of a .45 caliber Colt semiautomatic.

"Aghhh," Smoke said after the blow.

"Drive!"

Smoke did as he was instructed. He closed the doors and pulled off.

"Where are we—" *Plap!* He received another physical warning. The car swerved into oncoming traffic, but he quickly recovered.

"Drive slowly. I'll tell you the turns," Samara reiterated.

Smoke had to make some decisions and fast. With the aggressiveness of the person in the backseat, he knew he was soon going to be in a dark alley waiting for someone to come and retrieve his body. If he made a scene and wound up getting the cops involved, he might get shot and live, but with the two guns under the seat, he would be going to jail for life. Especially since his gun was used in both shootings at the center. That left one other alternative.

"Right!" Samara grunted.

Smoke proceeded to the next intersection and made a right. He knew what he had to do. He only needed a small window of opportunity.

"Right at the alley," she said.

Smoke knew the moment of truth was at hand.

Samara could have ended the ordeal when they first got into the car. The silencer could have put him out of his misery before he knew that someone was behind him, but she wanted him to suffer a little bit by anticipating his death. She had already figured that he wasn't stupid enough to reach for the gun he thought was still under the seat. So that left him with three options. Bail when the car stopped. Bail while it was in motion. Or take his punishment like a man. She figured he'd try to do what he saw on TV hundreds of times and leap from the car while it was moving.

Smoke's heartbeat raced as his adrenaline climaxed. He had done a lot of crud in his lifetime, but he was determined not to go out like that. He turned slowly into the alley. Samara tried to decide whether to hit him before he tried to jump or to jump with him.

While she hesitated, he leaped from the car that was going about fifteen miles an hour. Samara was only a half second behind him. As he ran, ducking low and zigzagging to avoid giving his assailant an easy target, Samara focused on Smoke. She fired two shots, tagging the young man twice. He stumbled forward, and just as he began to fall, one last whisper from the .45 tapped him across the head. He hit the ground and took one last breath before he made his departure. Immediately after, Samara made hers.

Chapter Twelve

Go See The Doctor

*S*amara ran down the street chasing Smoke. When she got close enough, she tackled him. Samara punched him in the face viciously. Afterward, she got up and continued to kick and stomp on him until he stopped moving. She turned around to walk away.

"I'm sorry, Samara," a voice called out from behind her. She turned to see Smoke standing with his hands in front of him pleading like a child trying to avoid a butt whooping. "It wasn't my fault. It won't happen again."

Samara extracted a gun and hit the young man twice in the chest. He collapsed. She began to turn around when she noticed him spring back to life as if yanked up by invisible strings. "I'm sorry. It wasn't my fault."

Suddenly the young man who was in the car with Smoke before she kidnapped him appeared and approached Samara with a knife. She fired two more shots, hitting both of them between the eyes. She watched their lifeless bodies fall to the ground.

Within seconds the young men were lifted to their feet and began to beg her not to kill them. Two more young men appeared out of nowhere brandishing handguns. She tagged all four young men across the head.

She did not turn around, but waited for the young men to rise up. A few seconds later, all four young men were on their feet. Samara looked into the sky above their heads and saw a huge man dangling the young men like they were puppets. The man was Caucasian, bald, and wearing a suit and tie. His nametag read The Man. He laughed continually at the young men's and Samara's actions.

Now there were four young men pleading for their lives, and four more with machine guns coming for her. Samara, seeing that she was in a situation in which she could not prevail, placed her gun on the ground.

All of the young men stood silently. The four with the machine guns placed them on the ground. The Man was very upset. He began to yank at their invisible strings. The entire group began fighting against each other.

Samara picked up her gun. All of the young men stopped fighting. The Man smiled. She began firing at The Man. Four of the young men grabbed their automatic guns and began firing at The Man too. The others picked up rocks and hurled them at him.

The Man seemed irritated at the bullets and rocks as if they were mosquitoes biting him. He picked up a huge gavel with "The System" engraved on it and smashed all eight young men into the ground. The Man began to laugh. Samara was horrified.

Samara turned around and prepared to run away from the gavel that was being turned on her. She turned to see her father and another young man run up to her and pull her away from the gavel that came crashing down.

After they were out of harm's way, Rufus pulled out a sniper rifle and executed The Man. He was immediately replaced by another man and the gavel was set back in motion. Rufus executed two more, but they were back in the same situation. A new The Man and gavel also known as The System were once again looking to smash all of them.

Rufus and Samara fired at the gavel to no avail. The young man, who was in his teens and favored Samara in appearance, stepped forward. She looked on in amazement.

As the gavel came fast and hard in an attempt to destroy them, Samara and Rufus attempted to grab the young man and run for cover, but he shrugged them off. The gavel was seconds away from obliterating them when the young man held up an open palm facing the sky, forcing the gavel to stop in mid-air about twenty feet over their heads. The Man, very confused as to what was happening, tried very hard to move the gavel, but it would not budge.

Then the young man waved his hand upward and his motion forced the gavel to hit The Man in the head, knocking him out. The young man raised a clenched fist in the air, the same as seen on black power logos of past, causing the gavel to explode. Samara and Rufus couldn't believe their eyes.

The young man walked back over to them with a blank expression on his face. Out of nowhere millions of people appeared and followed him in awe and silence.

"Who are you?" Samara asked.

"Ma, what are you talking about?" he asked.

Samara awoke from her dream shivering. She wasn't sure what to make of it. The first half of the dream seemed obvious to her. Despite the fact that she had made her city a better place by smoking Smoke's boots, somewhere deep down inside she regretted it. Moreover, she concluded that by killing him, she had participated in The Man's plan to divide, kill, and destroy her and her people. But she didn't understand who the young man was, the power he held, or why he had called her Ma.

Samara rolled out of her bed, knocking her vibrator on the floor, and grabbed the telephone. She dialed her mother's number.

"Hello," Natalie, Samara's mother, answered.

"Good morning, Ma."

"Hey, baby. How are you?"

"I'm holding on. I need to talk to you."

"Sure, sweetie. What do you want to talk about?"

"I'm on my way."

"OK. Did you eat anything yet?"

"No."

"I'll see you soon," Natalie said as they both got off the phone.

About a half hour later Samara arrived at her mother's house just off of Pennsylvania Avenue in Southeast. She pulled out her key and let herself in. As soon as she stepped through the door, her mother stood waiting with open arms. They gave each other a big hug.

"Where's Marcus?"

"You know your brother. His lazy ass is still up there in the bed," Natalie said as she headed toward the living room to take a seat on the couch. Samara followed her and sat as well.

"If I didn't have more pressing issues on my mind, I would go and drag him up out of that bed. He was an hour and a half late the other day."

Natalie shook her head. "So what's on your mind, Maury?"

Samara let out a deep sigh. "Ma, you know how Daddy raised me."

"All too well. We had many a fight about him training my little angel into GI Jane. Teaching you to defend yourself is one thing, but he was teaching you how take out a small army by yourself." The truth was, Natalie really didn't have a clue as to all the things her husband had taught Samara. Samara's mother went ballistic when she found out that her husband had taught their baby girl how to handle, clean, and fire handguns and rifles prior to her tenth birthday.

"It wasn't like that," Samara said with a slight smile.

"Whatever."

"He taught me some principles too, Ma. Unfortunately, I had to use one of them last night," Samara said, looking down at the floor.

Natalie placed her finger under Samara's chin, lifting and turning her head so that they were eye to eye.

"Samara . . . what happened?"

Samara paused as tears glistened in her eyes. "Ma, there was this man a little older than me, and . . ." She paused again.

Thoughts began racing through Natalie's head. She started to assume the conversation was about a relationship. Maybe her daughter was pregnant.

"It's OK, baby. Let it out."

"He was bad. I mean really, really bad. He had no respect for anyone, including children." Samara went on to tell her the whole story from the time Donté warned her about Smoke until the second shooting inside the center. She also told her about the time he opened fire on her.

"That's one evil son of a bitch. He opened fire on women and children and said F the children and shot

at my baby twice? I hope that bastard is behind bars."
Natalie was a very calm person and few things could
move her to anger to the point of profanity, except
Rufus.

"Actually he's dead, Ma."

"Well what's the problem?" Samara looked into her
mother's eyes. She was on the verge of crying, but managed to hold back the tears by looking at the ceiling
and blinking. "Maury?"

"Yes?"

"Did you . . ."

Samara nodded, indicating that she was responsible
for taking him out. Natalie reached over and gave Samara a huge embrace. Samara explained what happened
during the hours leading up to his death.

"Maury, I understand that he was very bad and you
were very mad, but you can't go around killing people
like you're a vigilante or something. If you're defending yourself, that's one thing, but to stalk, kidnap, and
kill is evil, Samara. Let God take care of people like
him. Eventually he would have gotten his."

Samara's look of sadness turned to frustration.

"I understand what you're saying, Ma, but eventually was unacceptable. He was going to come back
again."

"Well why didn't you tell the police—Rufus?"

Samara shook her head. "I know I act like Daddy.
But I'm like you, too. I wanted to take him out after he
shot those folks outside the center. After he shot at me,
that was an automatic death sentence, but thinking of
you and the things you taught me, I tried to find a reason to save his life. After he barged into the center and
shot at women and children, it was out of my hands."

"Samara, you've accomplished so much. I just don't

want you to throw your life away for someone like that. Besides, I thought you opened the center to help people like him."

"I did. I didn't feel that bad about it before, but I had a dream last night and it showed me that deep down I have some regrets about what I did. I just came to get some encouraging words from you."

"And shake your daddy off of you," Natalie interjected.

"Ma?"

Natalie threw up her hand. "When is the last time you've been to church?"

"I've been so busy with school and the center, I—"

"I didn't ask for excuses," Natalie interrupted. "I asked for an approximate date." Samara looked away before answering.

"Probably a year or so?"

"What!" Natalie was incensed. "Girl, are you out of your mind?"

"Ma, after Daddy disappeared, I went to church and prayed every single Sunday. After he was gone for about a year, I just gave up."

"Maury, you're on God's time and not the other way around. His will is divine. No matter what happens, you can never give up on God. He's never given up on you. Look how he's blessed you. What you need to realize is that the devil hasn't given up on you either. If he can separate you from God, he can take away all that you have and he can take you out. Don't ever forget that."

Samara looked like a small child that had been scolded.

"Samara?" Natalie called. Her daughter faced her. "Go on and get your mind right by getting back in church. You came to me for some encouraging words, and there you have 'em."

* * *

Later that evening Craig convinced Samara to go out on another date. They had spent a little more time together since their first date. They went to the movies a few times and out to eat. He was slowly working his way into her heart, even though she kept true to her word and never allowed him a second kiss.

Samara needed to get her mind off of the things that had transpired over the last couple of days. Craig had spent a lot more time with her and at the center after the first shooting. He always found a way to cheer her up, and that night she really needed it.

They went out to eat at TGI Friday's, a restaurant located on Pennsylvania Avenue in Northwest near George Washington University. Craig could see that Samara was still not herself, and he assumed it was because of the shootings. He made light jokes and small talk, and managed to get her to loosen up a bit.

"You want to catch a movie tonight?" Craig asked.

"I don't really feel like it tonight."

Craig nodded. "I understand. How about we catch a movie at my place? I got a hell of a DVD collection."

She eyed him suspiciously. "I don't care. Just make sure you keep your hands to yourself," she said with a weak smile.

Craig's eyes bulged wide. He couldn't believe she had agreed to come to his place. He expected a no with a lot of sass behind it. She really wasn't herself that day. He had to see how far he could push it.

"Check, please," Craig said quickly. He had heard all that he needed to hear.

On the way to his apartment he said the sweetest things possible and held her hand the entire time. Inside the apartment Samara noticed that it was very clean. In fact, it was too clean for a bachelor or anyone with masculinity. She took note of it and sat on the nicely maintained leather couch. As corny as it seemed to Samara at the time, Craig put on the movie *Love and Basketball*.

Before the movie was halfway through, they were hugged up on the couch with Craig continuously pecking her on the cheek. By the end of the movie he managed to get a kiss, tongue to tongue, that lasted for nearly five minutes.

Samara knew what Craig's intentions were when he asked her to come over. She was really considering Tonya's prescription for stress relief. She just didn't know whether she could go through with it. By the end of the movie and with all the moves Craig had put on her, she had resolved within herself to let it go and see what happened.

The kissing led to fondling and the fondling to undressing. They were in their undergarments admiring each other. Craig was fully erect when he pulled down his underwear and revealed to Samara what looked like a pole. He could see she was impressed. He removed her bra and began sucking on her perfectly shaped breasts. He placed a finger on her crotch before quickly removing her panties.

As he tried to place his body on top of hers, she pushed him away. She stared at him intensely. He looked confused at first, but then he ran into his bedroom and returned with a condom.

"You were surely about to mess it up," Samara said.

"I was just caught up in the heat of the moment. My bad. But actually I am about to fuck it up."

Chapter Thirteen

Love Yourself

Samara woke up the next morning feeling worse than she did the day before. Immediately after her session with Craig, she ordered him to take her home. Craig was a little confused and upset behind the request. Most women would be begging to stay the night, yet she was insisting to go. He was upset because he had every intention of seeing her a few more times during the course of the night.

Craig knew he had taken care of her body. There was no doubt about that. He couldn't understand what had happened between her reaching her climax and a few minutes later when she was fully dressed and ready to go.

As soon as Samara got home she took a long, hot bath in an attempt to wash her sin away. When she got out of bed a couple of hours later, she took a shower, the second time she had bathed in less than five hours. Soap and water were not enough to wash away the disdain she had with herself.

Although she felt like she was in heaven while they

were doing it, she felt horrible when it ended. She had promised herself years ago that the only time she would ever consider having sex again was with some- one she loved. She and Craig were not at that point. She allowed lust, a deceitful and dangerous emotion, to take control of her, and she felt violated afterward.

Not only did Samara feel like she had let herself down, but she also felt like she had let down the young ladies she had been coaching the last few weeks to have more respect for their bodies. It was so hypocriti- cal. She had been fervently preaching abstinence, and then she gave herself away to assuage the remorse of committing murder. And to add insult to injury, she was set to host a day-long conference on abstinence that very day.

Samara arrived at the center an hour before it was set to open. She prepped the large conference room for the event. She did everything in her power to shake off the foolishness of the night before and get inspired about helping the young women to love themselves.

About a half hour later Tonya showed up.

"What's up, girl?" Tonya asked, smiling. Samara rolled her eyes. "Oops. What was all that about?" Samara just shook her head. "Excuse me. I asked, 'What was all that about?'" Tonya reiterated with her hands on her hips.

"I'm having side effects."

"What? What are you talking about?"

"That prescription you called in."

Tonya eyes glowed with amazement. "Maury, you gave him some?" Samara put her head down and nod- ded. "Girl, I never thought you would go through with it, especially no time soon."

"And I shouldn't have."

"Why? It wasn't good? Is he with the itty bitty com- mittee? What happened?"

"It isn't that. He's toting and the sex was wonderful."

"Well what the hell is the problem?"

Samara sighed. "For casual sex, I have a vibrator. If I have a partner that's because I'm in love, and that wasn't the case last night. I abandoned my morals to try and stave off guilt."

"What guilt?"

Samara proceeded to tell one of the only other people in the world she trusted besides her parents and Marcus about the events that led up to Smoke's demise. Tonya was a little surprised, but not very.

"He deserved it."

"He did, but I felt guilty all the same. And I used that guilt as an excuse to lower my standards. Now I have to preach to these young ladies not to do the same stuff I'm guilty of doing."

"We'll do fine, Maury." Just the fact that Tonya acknowledged that they were in it together made her feel better. Samara nodded and smiled.

"Don't think about yourself right now. Think about the fact that you may be saving some young girl a lot of pain and misery, and maybe even her life. You made a mistake," she said before mumbling, "at least in your eyes." Samara heard Tonya and playfully pushed her. They both laughed. "You made a mistake. So what? Everyone does, even Samara Brown. As a leader you have to shake it off and continue to lead.

"It was probably a good thing it happened. Now you can come at them as someone who's been in their shoes, instead of prescribing remedies for things you know little to nothing about. Maury, everything will be fine."

Samara smiled at Tonya.

"You're right."

"I know. I usually am," Tonya said matter-of-factly.

"Except when it comes to men and having casual sex."

Tonya put her finger over her lips, motioning for Samara to keep quiet as if someone else were in the building and could hear them. They laughed off the situation and continued setting up the room.

The workshop was elaborately crafted. It included all females ages ten and older, although Samara and Tonya personally went to the parents of girls under thirteen to receive permission for them to attend and invited the parents as well. She had players from the Washington Wizards and the Redskins in attendance. Also attending were a nationally renowned ObGyn and a local comedian who had just been in a nationally released movie. Samara had an all-star cast to drive home the point that the young women needed to respect their bodies.

Midway through the program, the star running back for the Redskins, Clyde Davis, talked with the young girls. The girls could hardly stop screaming over having the celebrity in their presence. After he motioned for them to quiet down, he took the floor.

"How are you young ladies doing this morning?" The words "fine" and "good" roared through the room.

"This is a beautiful program and I'm very happy to be a part of it. I don't know if Ms. Brown is going to allow it, but I'ma have to keep it real in here," he said, looking over to Samara. Tonya had been smiling since the seven-time Pro Bowl football player entered the room, and she had been flirting hard ever since. Just as he looked over at Samara, Tonya waved for the third time. Samara smiled, bowed, and motioned with her hand to officially give him the floor.

"I'm here to bring you young ladies the other side of the equation. As a man, my perspective is a little different from the ladies who gave you reasons to abstain, because most men, young and old, don't want females to abstain unless they're their daughters or grand-daughters or nieces.

"See, people as a whole have become more and more selfish. You see sex on network television and PG-13 movies nowadays. Most of your advertisements feature half naked women in them. Almost every music video you see, whether it's a male rapper or a female singer, has women with little to no clothes on shaking their butts. Sex sells, as they say. What most people don't re-alize is that what it sells often times is your soul." At that point into his speech he had everyone's attention, even Tonya's. Samara, who had spoken briefly with him, didn't realize he was so poignant.

"Let me explain something to y'all. Do you know what puts most people in jail?"

"Police," was the unanimous response from the crowd. Clyde laughed.

"I asked what, not who." The audience laughed. "The thing that puts most people in jail is the same thing that turns people into drug addicts. It's the same thing that causes people to contract sexually transmitted diseases like AIDS. It's the same thing that causes a teenager to become pregnant."

Clyde paused for a moment. The audience waited impatiently for the answer to the world's ills. Then he dropped it on them.

"No self-control. Not having any self-control is the reason teenagers become pregnant. Lack of self-control is the reason that people get AIDS from having unpro-tected sex. Not being able to control yourself will lead you to drugs or jail. A life without self-control is a wasted life.

"Playing football takes a lot of control and self-discipline. In order to achieve your goals or be good at anything, you have to have discipline. Without control, you'll never become anything, and you'll let others control you. Do y'all understand?"

Many in the crowd nodded in agreement. A few people said yes. He continued.

"People who couldn't control themselves are on drugs right now being controlled by the drugs and drug dealers. People who couldn't control their actions and their bodies are being controlled by a disease without a cure that kills you slowly and painfully.

"You see, males, boys, and men are simple. We see, we like, and we go after. After we see what we like, we want to try it out. We're not really concerned about feelings or what you may like. All of that small talk is a means to an end. That end is to get into your pants."

There was murmuring in the crowd. The women were nodding and saying yup. The teenagers giggled amongst each other, and those younger than them said awww as if someone had cursed aloud.

"I'm going to close with this. Men don't respect women who give up their bodies easily. I know there are women who say there's a double standard because men can sleep with dozens of women and be applauded, while if a woman does that, then she is looked upon as a slut. That argument is stupid. Just because a man isn't that smart and thinks with his lower head, a woman shouldn't lower herself to his level and give him what he wanted in the first place in the name of getting even. If women have more self-control, men wouldn't have so many partners. Put sex in its place—first love, then marriage, and then sex. Love yourself and wait."

Clyde left the podium to a standing ovation and applause. Marcus gave him a gentle bump.

"You trying to make me give in my player's card?" Marcus asked him, smiling.

"I just want you to make better decisions, brother." They shook hands.

"I never expected to hear that from a star football player."

"I've been that man who went through women, but I've grown up. All that looks good isn't good for you, brother. I've had to chase some of my sister's male friends away when I was younger, and now I've got a daughter. She's only five, but I know she's going to have a lot of men chasing her, and I want her to be prepared if she meets someone like you." They both laughed. "I'm just kidding. I don't want her to meet someone like the person I used to be, or someone like most of my teammates are—married or not. They come at my daughter with the bullshit, I got a twelve-gauge locked and loaded. Did you see *Player's Club* when Jamie Foxx met LisaRaye's father? That's going to be me."

Marcus just nodded, listening closely.

Samara took the podium.

"We're about to conclude our program. I was supposed to give a little speech in closing, but after Clyde just put it down like that, there isn't much more to be said. I'm just going to say a few words and let y'all go.

"Young ladies, have some dignity about yourselves. Your body is a temple. It's sacred. It's worth more than any clothes, jewelry, or money. Your body is not to be trifled with, used, and abused at someone else's discretion. I'm guilty of making mistakes, too, but I've learned that my body and my health are important to me, too important to give my time and energy to someone who only cares about my body and what I can do for his.

"Y'all have seen the pictures. You've heard the horror stories. Having unprotected sex is equivalent to playing Russian roulette, and with the rate of HIV infections being so high in DC, you're more likely to get hit than missed. It's not worth it. The only true prevention is abstinence. If you have to bring yourself down and have sex before you're married, he needs to have a condom, or he needs to wait. To hell with him. Love yourself."

Chapter Fourteen

My Favorite Trollop

A few days later Samara was taking care of some paperwork concerning the employees' payroll when a beautiful but scantily clad young woman named Stacy entered her office. There was obvious distress on her face.

"Ms. Brown, I need to talk you."

Samara put the paperwork away. "Certainly, have a seat." The young woman sat in the chair in front of the desk opposite Samara. Even after she sat down, she seemed very anxious. "Calm down. Tell me your name and what's on your mind," Samara said.

"My name is Diamond," she said without looking up.

"Is that what your mother named you?"

"No. My real name is Stacy Smith." Samara nodded.

"Ms. Brown, this is a really nice facility."

"Thank you."

"This is only my second time here."

Samara wanted her to get to the point, but she could see the lady needed to feel comfortable before she opened up, so she began to small talk with her.

"Really? When was the first?"

"The other day when you had that conference about abstinence," she said, making eye contact before looking down at the desk again.

"Did you like it?"

"I loved it. I wish I could have heard it ten years ago." Samara nodded.

The door to Samara's office opened suddenly and Marcus entered.

"Didn't I tell you to knock before busting in here?" Samara asked.

"My bad, sis. I thought you were alone. I'll come back." Marcus and Stacy held each other's gazes for a few seconds before he left.

"Where were we? Oh, yeah. How old are you?" Samara asked.

"Nineteen."

"Ms. Smith?" Samara asked.

Stacy looked up innocently. The only people who called her that in the last few years were police officers and judges. "Whatever you want to talk to me about, I'm here. If I can help you in any way through whatever trouble you're going through, I will."

Stacy smiled and nodded. "Ms. Brown, I'm a whore. I sleep with three to ten men every night. I had slept with seven the night and morning before the conference. I've been hooking since I was fifteen. I had sex with an associate of my crack smoking mother who was fifteen years older than me. He bought me all these nice things at first. Within a few months he was my pimp and I was turning tricks for him.

"I never in my wildest dreams thought that I would grow up to become a prostitute. I hate my lifestyle and I hate my life." Samara wanted to interject at that point, but she thought it would be better to let Stacy vent. "These men treat me like I'm not even a human being. They treat me like a mindless robot, or a slave. I'm just flesh for them to stick their nasty and smelly things wherever they please. Some of my regular clients are politicians and policemen and business-men, and they ain't shit. None of them even take off their wedding rings. And the way they talk to me is ridiculous." Tears began to form in her eyes.

"I can't take it anymore. I tried to quit about a year ago, but my pimp beat me so badly that I couldn't work for nearly a week, and he threatened to kill me if I 'ever started thinking again.' I haven't worked the streets since the conference, and Joe has been looking high and low for me. He's told people I don't work for him anymore. He tells them I'm dead, but he just hasn't found the body yet.

"Ms. Brown, I'm homeless, hungry, and don't have any money or clothes. All of the clothes I owned are at Joe's. All the things I have in this world are with me right now. I need help, Ms. Brown. Please!" she said before tears began to flow.

Samara got up and walked around the desk. She gave Stacy a big hug.

"The most important things you have now that you didn't have before are your dignity and freedom. Stacy, whatever you need, I got you."

Stacy looked up at her, smiled, and said, "Thank you," before returning Samara's embrace.

"Let's go and meet Tonya, get something to eat, and get you a bath and some clothes." Stacy smiled again and hugged Samara even tighter.

"Thank you, Ms. Brown."

"Girl, I'm only two years older than you. Call me Maury." They both smiled before exiting the office.

Samara and Stacy rode around the neighborhood in Samara's car like a pair of old friends who had just gotten reacquainted. They picked up some fast food on the way to Samara's place. Samara and Stacy were almost the same size, so Samara let her put on one of her outfit's after bathing. Then they went to Macy's and picked up a few outfits for her. After leaving the mall they headed back to the center with Stacy's new outfits and shoes in the trunk of the car.

"Since you've been out there since you were fifteen, I'ma guess you don't have a diploma or GED?" Samara asked. Stacy shook her head, indicating that she didn't.

"It's cool. We have a partnership with an organization that can help you get your GED. And I have a surprise for you."

Stacy was wondering what more Samara could give her. She had already helped her escape a life of sexual slavery and had given her new clothes and a place to stay. She even gave her fifty dollars to put in her pocket. It was more money than Joe had ever allowed her to have. What more could she possibly do for her?

"I got a job for you at the center."

"What? Are you sure?"

"Absolutely. You're a very sweet young lady. It would be a blessing to have you work at the center."

Stacy's eyes were becoming watery.

"Thank you so much, but why are you doing all of this for me?"

"Because I love you. You remind me of good friends who made mistakes and aren't here anymore. I wish I could have helped them and any other black person that wants to be helped. That's what the center is all about. We have to get these youth to want to do something and be somebody while they're still young and impressionable. We need leaders and we need a place to start cultivating them. I can think of no better place than the hood." They both laughed.

They arrived at the center a few minutes later, laughing and joking like junior high school girls. No sooner than they got out of the car they were approached by an older man wearing too much bling. His hat and suit were cliché from an era a few decades earlier—the time of infamy for the black pimp that preceded and proceeded a host of blaxplotation movies.

"Diamond." He called to her from about thirty feet away and closing. In a much lower tone and halfway laughing, he continued, "You stinking bitch. Do you know how much money you done cost me?"

Samara could tell by his appearance that this was Joe. Samara sized him up to be about five feet eight, a 160 pounds, and not physically fit. She looked at Stacy, who had snuck behind her, cringing. Stacy was absolutely terrified, shivering like she had seen a ghost.

Joe was up on them now.

"Hey, beautiful," he said to Samara. She frowned so hard it looked like she had just sucked a lemon. He dismissed her with a wave of his hand. Joe attempted to reach around Samara to grab Stacy. In one motion Samara placed her hand on his chest and pushed him away so hard that he stumbled, nearly falling.

Joe looked down at his chest, stunned that she had put her hands on him. He looked up at her and was amazed at how strong she was.

"Bitch, I know you did not just put your hand on me."

"The only bitch out here is the one who just got pushed. I'm going to suggest you be on your way before you get yourself embarrassed out here."

Joe was shocked even more by her boldness. He lunged forward with a wild hook. Samara sidestepped him like he was moving in slow motion. Before he could regain his bearings and throw another wild and weak punch, she kicked him in the groin. Once he leaned over in excruciating pain, she pulled her right hand over her left shoulder and back slapped him so hard the sound could be heard a block away. He stumbled and fell over.

"If you ever see this young lady again, you go in the opposite direction. If you look at her the wrong way or say a word to her, good or bad, I'm coming to see you and I'm not going to be so nice next time." She stomped him in the face twice, causing him to collapse back to the ground. She leaned over and checked his waist and pockets to make sure he didn't have a gun on him. She retrieved a pocketknife.

Samara walked over to Stacy who was beyond words. Over the past few years she had seen Joe handle many women like that, but never thought she would see him handled that way by a woman. Samara looked Stacy in the eyes.

"You don't have to be scared of assholes like that. We're going to teach you some self-defense while you're here too. You've just been completely emancipated from the street life. You're a brand new person, here to help others just as I have helped you."

While Samara was talking a few people from inside the center came outside, including Tonya, Marcus, and Donté. Marcus and Donté were running. Samara left Stacy's side to intercept her brother and her apprentice. She grabbed Marcus, but Donté slipped past.

"Tay!" Samara yelled. He stopped midway into delivering more punishment to the pimp. "I've already taken care of the situation. Just make sure he leaves."

Donté forced Joe to his feet.

"Get your bitch-ass up. If you come back around

here again you going have to see me," Donté said, ushering him away.

"What's going on, sis?" Marcus asked. "I got people running up to me saying, 'your sister is outside fighting.'"

"There wasn't a fight. I just had to slow him down."

"Who is that?" Marcus asked.

"I'll explain to you later."

"Some man comes and tries to put his hands on my sister? Hell, naw, you need to tell me now."

"Who are you talking to, Marcus Calvin? I'm the big sister," Samara said. She paused and took a deep breath. "He wasn't trying to fight me."

Marcus looked over at Stacy. Stacy looked down at the ground. Marcus understood what was going on. He left Samara and Stacy and walked in the direction of Donté and Joe.

"Marcus," she called to him. Without looking back he held up his hand, basically telling her to save it. They forced Joe into his Cadillac L Dog. Both young men had some harsh words for Joe as he pulled off.

Chapter Fifteen

Bamboozled

The center had it bumps and bruises since its inception, but now it was rolling. It was July Fourth, and Samara had set up another grand celebration comparable to the one on opening day. She had the grills set up, Moon Bounces, and games for all to enjoy. Everyone was having a beautiful time.

Samara, Stacy, and Tonya stood near the dunk machine, hoping someone would hit the bullseye and dunk Marcus. It took Samara nearly fifteen minutes to get him to agree to participate. The conditions he required were that Samara couldn't throw the ball, and he wanted twenty dollars in cash, up front. The ladies laughed at the nervous expression on Marcus's face as little Cindy nearly dropped him into the water.

Donté walked over to the ladies.

"Hey, Tay, are you going to relieve my brother?" Samara asked.

"Hell no!" They all giggled.

"These kids couldn't hit a brick wall," Tonya said. "Go ahead and have some fun."

"Besides, it's ninety degrees out here," Stacy added. "A little water won't hurt."

Donté looked each woman in the eyes before stopping at Samara.

"Do y'all think I'm stupid? I know before I sit down good Maury is gonna be tossing that ball at the target and putting me in that dirty looking water. I don't know how you bamboozled Marcus to get up there."

"He made me agree not to throw the ball. He also required me to pay him. What he doesn't realize is that since I had to pay him that negated me not participating. I have to get my money's worth," Samara replied. They all began to laugh. Donté shook his head. Samara produced a softball.

"Where'd you get that from?" Donté asked.

"I had to sneak it. If he sees me paying for some balls to throw at him, he might try to get out. By the time he realizes what's going on, he'll be cursing me out— underwater," Samara said with a wicked grin.

"You're terrible," Donté replied.

She smiled.

Little Cindy had just missed her third attempt. Samara hurried to the area where participants stood. Marcus saw his sister, heard a clink, a swoosh, and he was submerged and pissed. Everyone in the vicinity burst into laughter. He got out of the water and stormed out of the contraption.

"What the hell was that?" Marcus asked, approaching his sister with a frown.

Samara was still laughing hard as she looked at the water running down his face. When she finally got herself together she responded.

"She steps up to pitch. She throws. Streeeike." Samara, Tonya, Stacy, and Donté laughed even harder.

MC walked away and returned a moment later with

a strap across his chest that was attached to something on his back.

"You know, I thought you might renege, so I bought some insurance with me," Marcus said before he whipped out a high powered water gun called the Super Soaker, and aimed it at Samara.

"Marcus!" Samara said just as her brother released a hard stream of water in her face. She turned and ran away as he continued soaking her. Stacy, Tonya, and Donté laughed at Samara.

After the water pressure was gone and Samara had fled the scene, MC started pumping more air into the chamber, which forced out the water when he depressed the trigger.

"Y'all thought it was funny when she dunked me, right?" Before they could protest, he hosed them all down, and they all dispersed.

Samara regrouped by taking a few balloons from the man blowing them up with helium and filling them with water. Samara crept up behind Marcus and called his name. Once he turned around, she hit him in the face with a water balloon. Before he could regroup and pump up his water gun, he caught a second balloon across the head. As he wiped his face, Samara disappeared.

Samara caught up with Donté.

"Bamboozled, huh?" He tried to escape, but she caught him across the back with her last balloon.

"It's on," Donté said. For the next two hours everyone participated in a large scale water fight. Kids, teenagers, young adults, and old were in on the fun.

With her hair still wet and her clothes clinging to her body, Samara was approached by two white women, one in her forties, and the other about college aged.

"Ms. Brown?" the older woman inquired. Samara

was clearly apprehensive and did not respond at first. "Are you Samara Brown?" the woman asked again.

"I am."

The older lady extended her hand.

"Hello. My name is Marsha Simms, and this is Jane Russell. We represent Change for Urban America and we're very impressed with you and your center."

Samara accepted the handshake and said, "Thank you."

"Absolutely. We love what you were able to do with this building and in this community." Samara nodded. "We're looking to expand our DC chapter, and we would love to be a part of this center." Samara looked at the woman as if she were crazy. Tonya walked onto the scene ready to hit Samara with a water balloon, but she paused when she saw Samara's facial expression as she conversed with the women.

"Be a part of the center?" Samara asked.

"Yes. We currently have over thirty volunteers and a host of programs I think you would love. Along with the little programs you already have set up, I think we can do a lot of good in this community," Ms. Simms said.

"Is that right?" Samara asked with a look of concern on her face. Tonya shared the expression. Ms. Simms and Ms. Russell nodded affirmatively. A small crowd began to form around them, wondering what had caused the pause in the water fight.

"Well I appreciate the offer, but I'm going to have to decline."

Ms. Simms and Ms. Russell both looked surprised, but Ms. Simms' face bordered on anger.

"Huh?" was the only response Ms. Simms was able to utter.

"Yup. We're good down here, but we appreciate the

offer. I wish you good luck with your organization and your programs. Now if you'll excuse me," Samara said, turning away. Ms. Simms caught her by the arm. Out of reflex Samara swung around, and less than two seconds after Ms. Simms grabbed her arm, Samara's hand was within inches of grabbing Ms. Simms by the throat. Luckily Samara was able restrain herself.

"Ma'am, I suggest that you turn me loose."

Ms. Simms let her arm go, surprised at the sudden violence she had exposed herself to.

"May I speak with you in private?" Ms. Simms asked.

"You may not. My answer is final." She moved in close to Samara.

"Look, I don't want to fight about this. We're all on the same team. We just want to help."

"Help who, Ms. Simms?"

"You people," Ms. Simms said, realizing her slip of the tongue a half second after the words slipped from her lips. "I mean your community."

Samara was initially outraged, but she heard what she wanted—the truth. She nodded.

"I thought so."

"I didn't mean it like that."

"Oh, you meant it. You just didn't plan on verbalizing it. It's cool, though."

"Look, Ms. Brown, I didn't want to fight, but if you're going to be difficult, I can make this really ugly for you. I know people," Ms. Simms said with a stern look to back up her threat. Samara smiled.

"Good, because I know people too," Samara said and backed away. "Hey, everybody," she yelled to the crowd that had formed. "This is Ms. Simms and Ms. Russell. Ms. Simms has just informed me that they would like to join our water fight. Let's welcome them to the fun."

Before Ms. Simms could protest, Tonya hit her in the face with a water balloon. Within seconds both ladies were drenched and running for cover. A few minutes later some police officers, along with Ms. Simms and Ms. Russell, found Samara, who was about to hurl a water balloon. One of the officers was Officer Presto, the female officer who had words with Samara on the center's opening day. Another crowd formed around them.

"Did you assault this woman?" the female officer asked.

"I did not."

"She said that you and your friends attacked her with water guns and balloons."

"She walked into the middle of a water fight that had been going on for hours. Do you want to compare her one witness with all of mine?"

Officer Presto was visibly frustrated. "You better watch it, Ms. Brown."

"You better believe it," Samara said. She then looked at Donté and winked. Samara threw the water balloon and hit Donté in the chest. He hurled one in her direction, but it smacked the officer in the face. A full-scale water fight broke out with the officers in the midst. The officers, Ms. Simms, and Ms. Russell fled the scene as Samara laughed hysterically.

Talking to herself, Samara said, "I know people, too—a whole community."

Chapter Sixteen

Craig Joins the Shit List

It was a few days after Independence Day when Samara finally agreed to go out with Craig again. He had been begging for a date or at least some time to talk to her ever since their physical encounter. He made a couple of trips to the center to talk with her, but she pretty much ignored him. He knew something was wrong, but she hadn't told him what.

Craig dropped in on Samara at the center that day and caught her in a good mood, laughing and joking with some of the kids. He immersed himself inside the fun and was able to pull Samara away while she was still smiling. He convinced her to have a private conversation with him. They went into her office and closed the door.

There was a look of frustration on Craig's face as he began to speak.

"Did I do something wrong?" he asked.

"What do you mean?"

"I mean since we . . ." he paused to think of the right

words, "made love, you haven't had any time or conversation for me. What's the problem?"

"Made love? The problem is the sex was horrible and I don't have time." The look on Craig's face was beyond astonishment. He looked like he was going to have a heart attack. He stopped breathing for a few seconds. Samara smiled. "I'm just kidding. You handled yours for sure. There is no denying that."

Craig let out a huge sigh of relief.

"Girl, don't be playing with me like that. Playing with a man's pride like that can kill him." After a moment of silence, Craig continued. "So what's the problem?" He smiled before asking, "Did I beat it up too much?"

Craig had done things with Samara that he usually didn't do when handling a woman, including performing oral sex. He always figured his man was so big and his wind so long, it wasn't necessary. But he did everything in his power to make it a night to remember for her, even changing his pace from fast strokes to slow, long to deep and grinding ones. Most women he had sex with he just punished, and they always came looking for more. He wanted Samara to fall in love with him. Once he saw what sex was like with her, along with all the good times they had and her strength, he was definitely falling in love with her.

She pursed her lips before answering.

"You put it down, but don't let your head get too big." Craig nodded and smiled, staring at her and waiting for her to continue. "You see, I had been celibate for a good little while right before I gave into temptation."

Craig's facial expression changed quickly. He didn't like the way she referred to their encounter. It sounded religious. The very few times he was denied access to a female's body, religion had a strong hand in it, so he was hoping that she wasn't about to shut him out.

"I had gone through a rough couple of days," Samara continued. "I was angry, sad, and felt guilty. I tried the only thing I hadn't tried before to make me feel better. Even though the sex was good, it was a bad idea."

"Samara, I don't know how you feel about me, but I care deeply for you. I've had a crush on you since the beginning of school. I've been chasing and been chased by girls all my life. I've finally found a woman who represents everything I ever wanted in a mate, and all I want to do is spend time with her. As far as sex is concerned, we're both adults, and adults who feel the way we do about each other let their mates know through intimacy."

Samara wasn't sure whether he had rehearsed those words, or whether he had used them on different women at different times, but she was sure he had game. She was a pretty good judge of character, and although there was still something about him that she didn't like, she thought he was being sincere.

"Look, Craig, you're a very nice guy—"

Hearing that line caused Craig to speak out, fearing that rejection was on the horizon.

"I don't want to hear that shit. I need—"

Samara put up her hand, interrupting him. "Will you shut up and listen?" she asked. Craig gave her his undivided attention. "I was raised by my parents to have discipline and morals and not to make the mistakes of my peers, but to be a leader and a role model for them. You know the very next day I had to talk to these young ladies about abstinence when I had fornicated the night before? I like you, but I can't lower my standards in order to deal with you."

After hearing that, Craig knew it would be awhile before she allowed him to freak her again, but that was cool. After sampling the goods, he knew for sure it was worth waiting for, even if that wait was until marriage. He had plenty of sexual sparring partners until she was ready. Whatever it took to keep her in his life, he would do.

"That's fine. I really, I mean *really* enjoyed that night with you, but I can wait. I definitely respect your morals and discipline. Usually when I put on a woman what I put on you, they begin to stalk me, trying to do it any and everywhere. You, on the other hand, came across something that conflicted with your beliefs and cut it off altogether. I respect that. Not having sex is one thing. But not having your company and conversation is unacceptable. Don't do me like that."

Samara smiled. "I hear you. We can hang out together again. I just needed to get back my focus, so I didn't have time to socialize."

Craig nodded. "I understand. So can we socialize tonight?"

"I'll let you know."

"Good, I'll pick you up after work."

"Did you hear what I said?"

"I heard you and I understand. No means no. Anything short of no is a yes for me," Craig said, opening the door. Samara giggled and waved him off.

Just as Craig was about to exit, Donté entered. They nearly bumped into each other.

"What's up, Tay?" Where've you been?" Craig asked. "Chillin'."

Craig looked back at Samara, who was taking note of the conversation.

"I hear you. I'ma holla at you," Craig said before leaving.

Donté entered and closed the door behind him. He looked at Samara strangely.

"Samara, is that really your boyfriend? He doesn't really seem like your type."

"No, he's not my boyfriend. What would make you think that? And what exactly is my type?"

"Do you remember when we first met and I kept playing with you, and you offered me up?" Donté asked. Samara smiled and nodded, and Donté continued. "Then Craig came and pulled me to the side." She nodded again. "He told me you were his girl. Plus, he's always coming to see you and I see y'all leave together sometimes."

"We're just friends."

"I guess y'all hang out because you were both star basketball players for the same school," Donté said, smiling.

Returning the smile, Samara said, "That's all." After a pause Samara asked, "What do you mean he doesn't seem like my type? What exactly is my type?"

"Positive!" Donté said emphatically. "A better question would be how do I know him?'"

"That was next."

"He's the connect."

Samara squinted her eyes, not sure she had heard him correctly.

"What did you just say?"

"Yeah, that's what I said. He brings in all the weight from New York."

"Weed?"

"Crack and dope, too. He's got bricks of whatever you need. Before I met you and saw there was a better way, I used to get crack and weed from him on a regular. He usually keeps the good stuff, too."

Samara was heated. She had slept with the enemy.

She knew there was something about him that she didn't like, but she never imagined the reason was dope slinging. Donté could see her frustration.

"And I never thought you would be into pretty boys," Donté said to lighten her up some. She laughed.

"I don't like pretty boys. As a matter of fact, our next date is in that boxing ring." Samara shook her head in frustration. "I'ma get him."

Donté smiled. "I'm sure you will. Hey, look, since you've got such a poor choice in men, and since you think I'm too young for you, I've got just the man for you."

"Oh yeah? And who might that be?"

"My brother Mike. You remember I told you about him?"

Samara nodded. "You told me he was locked up, but didn't tell me why. I don't like to judge people before I meet them, but if he's in for selling drugs or gang activity, then I can assure you he's not my type." Donté smiled.

"You'll love him."

"What is he in for, Tay?"

"He's coming home soon. I'll let him tell you."

"How long has he been in?"

"Long enough. Like I said, I'll let him explain it to you."

Chapter Seventeen

And Don't You Come Back No More

Just outside the center, Craig pulled up in his Benz looking and smelling good. He had a wide grin on his face as he leaned on the front of the car. He watched as Samara, Tonya, Stacy, Donté, and Marcus exited and locked up the building.

"Who is that?" Stacy asked, looking at the well-dressed young man sitting on top of the expensive car.

"That's Samara's boyfriend," Tonya said matter-of-factly.

"The hell he is," Samara said.

"Whatever," Tonya responded. The group stopped just outside the building to talk.

"Marcus, here," Samara said, handing him the keys.

"What?" Marcus asked, looking over at Craig before turning his attention back to Samara. "You going out with him?"

"I am."

"Sis, when I first met him at the graduation he was OK, but there's something about him I don't like," Marcus said with a slight frown on his face.

"I know"—she paused before continuing—"me, too."

"Well why are you going out with him?"

"I'm going out tonight to straighten him out. I might need you to come pick me up later, because he might not want to bring me home when he hears what I have to say."

"Oh naw. In that case, I'm following you."

"Marcus," she said, tapping her purse, "I'm good." Marcus smiled. He knew that even without the gun in her purse she could handle the situation.

"Well what about Stacy?" he asked.

"What about me?" Stacy interjected.

"I was asking my sister," he said to Stacy before facing Samara. "How is Stacy getting home?"

"I think the question has already been answered," Stacy said. "Every night when I get off of work, the person driving that car"—Stacy pointed to Samara's Cadillac CTS—"drives me home, and since you have the keys . . ." Samara and Tonya laughed. As females they could see what was going on. Donté looked on curiously.

"I'm not taking you home," Marcus declared.

"Not right away. You can take me out until it's time to pick up your sister."

Marcus was visibly shaken by her words. The anxiety he attempted to conceal was out for all to see. Samara and Tonya snickered.

Donté shook his head in disappointment. He felt that he needed to bring Marcus up to speed because he was slipping. If Stacy had flirted with him that way while she was still hooking, he would've ignored her. But now that Samara got her mind right, she was a dime piece. Ever since Samara had convinced her to retire from the oldest profession, she wasn't giving men the time of day. She carried herself like a lady with so much dignity you would have never thought she had ever demeaned herself to prostitution. Donté knew that Marcus had better hop on that.

When Marcus was finally able to get himself together, he said, "Go out? I don't like you like that." Donté lowered and shook his head.

"Oh, you like me," Stacy said matter-of-factly. "Every time I try to get a look at you, I find you already staring at me. And besides," she said in a sweet and sincere voice, "I like you, Marcus Calvin." Samara and Tonya started laughing as Marcus stood there completely speechless.

Stacy walked over, put her arm inside of Marcus's, and then turned to Samara.

"What time should we pick you up, and where?" she asked.

Samara looked over at Craig, who immediately registered a look of frustration on his face. He pointed to his watch, letting her know she was taking too long. She dismissed him, waving the back of her hand at him. Samara turned her attention back to Stacy and smiled.

"I won't be that long. In fact, that car isn't going anywhere with me in it." She turned to Tonya. "Can you come get me in about twenty minutes, please?"

"Only if we go to the club tonight," Tonya said. Samara sighed.

"Whatever, Tonya." Samara turned her attention to Stacy and Marcus. "You guys have fun."

"We will," Stacy said for both of them. Stacy led Marcus to the car. A moment later they pulled off.

"I'll see y'all in the morning," Donté said to Samara and Tonya.

"Bye, sweetie," Tonya replied.

"Be safe," Samara added. Donté nodded and walked

away. He left their sight, but not the area. He had to keep an eye on his buddy Samara, and make sure Craig didn't get out of line.

"I got to tell you about Craig," Samara said to Tonya. "What?"

"I'll tell you when you come to pick me up." Tonya agreed and left. Samara finally made her way over to Craig's car. He smiled.

"You act like you ain't going to see them again," he said.

He opened the door for her and she got inside. He went around to the other side of the car and let himself in. He placed the key in the ignition, but before he could crank up the engine, she placed her hand on his arm, preventing him from turning the key.

He took his hand away from the ignition.

"What's the problem now, Samara?"

She leaned over like she was going to give him a kiss and feel him up, but instead she reached under the seat and extracted his gun. Before he could react, the gun was pointing at him.

"Girl, what are you doing?" he asked.

"I need for you to answer some questions. How you answer could be detrimental to your health."

"You better put that damn gun down, now!"

"Hey, Craig, I'm not playing with you." He calmed down a little. She started with a throw-off question. "Are you cheating on me?" She could care less whether he was or wasn't, but she wanted to feel him out so that she could decipher deception from him. He smiled.

"No, girl. I've got friends that happen to be female, but I haven't been out or had sex with anyone else but you." She knew that was a blatant lie as she carefully observed his body language. "Now go on and put that gun down."

"Why do you have a gun in your car?" He quickly formed a lie to give her, but a question suddenly dawned on him. How did she know he had a gun at all?

"I've been robbed twice since I came to this city. I'm paranoid." He frowned before asking, "How did you know I had a gun?"

"I'm asking the questions. You do the answering. Empty your pockets."

"You gonna rob me? You're gonna rob me with my own gun?"

"I'm not going to ask you again." He emptied his pockets and pulled out wads of money. It was easily a few thousand of dollars at first glance. He had a stack of large bills and a larger stack of smaller bills. "How much money is that?"

"Enough," he responded sarcastically.

"Where'd you get it?"

"From the bank."

"Are you a bank robber or a comedian?" He remained silent. "Or are you a dope boy?" He paused a second before answering.

"Ain't nobody selling no damn dope."

"You're right about that. I hope you quit voluntarily. You don't want me to get involved," Samara said, shaking her head.

"Who the fuck are you?"

"Don't find out the hard way. I don't want to see you again. Clean up your act. That's the only warning you're going to get."

"Look, Samara, I don't know what you think you know about me, but if you cut into my business, I will fuck you up. I like you, but don't take that for a weakness. If you get involved in attempting to undermine my business, you're likely to come up missing."

Samara nodded. She used her left hand to reach across her body and open the door. She eased out and put the gun in her purse.

"I hear you. I'm going to be in your business, and if you come looking for me, don't come alone."

Chapter Eighteen

Death Wish

Samara was sleeping soundly when her house phone rang. She arose and looked at the clock. It was nearly three in the morning. She had just turned in from a night of clubbing about an hour before. She let the phone ring until the answering machine picked up. Stacy's voice came on the line. She was hysterical and crying.

"Samara, Samara, please pick up the phone. Marcus got shot. Please pick—"

"What!" Samara asked after picking up the receiver and yelling through the phone.

"Marcus got shot," Stacy said again, still crying.

"Where are you?"

"Washington Hospital Center," Stacy said as she immediately heard a phone slam in her ear. Samara quickly put back on her clothes and was on her way out the door when she remembered that she needed to call her mother. After receiving no answer to the first call, she hung up and immediately called back. Her mother answered after the third ring.

"Ma, Marcus has been shot. Get Jesse and come to the Hospital Center."

"Oh no! How is he?"

"I don't know, Ma. I'm on my way to the hospital now. I'll see you there."

"We're on the way," her mother said as she hung up the phone.

Samara arrived at the hospital about ten minutes later. She went to the front desk and asked where her brother was. After she was given instructions, she went to the third floor. She saw Stacy sitting in a general waiting area sobbing. She rushed up to her.

"Where is he?" Samara asked. Stacy looked up, got up, and gave Samara a huge hug. Samara returned the embrace before moving her backward and asking, "Where is he?" for the second time in ten seconds.

Between sobs Stacy got out, "In surgery. We can't see him right now."

Samara placed her arm around Stacy's shoulder and they both sat down.

"Calm down and tell me what happened."

Stacy took a deep breath and paused for about a minute. "After we left the center we went to Friday's and got something to eat. We had a good time and good conversation. Your brother is intelligent and really sweet when he stops trying to act tough." They both smiled.

"I know," Samara responded.

"Afterward he asked did I want to go home. I told him no. He said, 'What do you want to do?' 'Have a good time,' I told him. He said, 'I got you,' and we went bowling."

Samara nodded and Stacy continued.

"We had so much fun. I hadn't had that much fun

since before I hit the streets. We laughed and joked and played. Both of us fell down the lane when he was trying to show me how to bowl," Stacy said through a very bright smile.

"What happened?" Samara was enjoying the story, but she needed to know how and why her brother was in the hospital. She was attempting to check herself, but she didn't know how she could possibly overlook an attempt on her brother's life. The assailants' best chance at survival was for them to be already incarcerated, or for Stacy to only be able to give a vague description of the attackers.

"We were just leaving when Troy and Big Stan were about to enter," Stacy said and paused as her eyes began to water again. For Samara the fact that Stacy knew them ruled out one of the things that may have saved their lives.

Seeing that Stacy was on the verge of breaking down Samara rubbed her back.

"It's OK. Just take your time." Samara paused for a few seconds. "Who are Troy and Big Stan?"

"Troy was a regular client of mine before I abruptly quit. Big Stan is his friend and the nephew of my former pimp." Samara shook her head.

"What happened?"

"Troy says, 'Damn, Diamond, where you been? Girl, I miss you.' Big Stan has this huge grin on his face and says, 'She tried to roll out on my uncle. Just thought she could pick up and walk away from being a whore. You cost my uncle a lot of money. When we bring her in, not only will we get a nice reward, he'll probably give you a few free sessions with her.'

"I tried to pull Marcus so we could get away, but he was pissed. Big Stan says to Marcus, 'Hey, slim, what's all the mugging for? This ain't got nothing to do with you. Go on and step off before you get yourself hurt.' And then Marcus said, 'You bitch-ass nigga, you ain't gonna do nothing to me.'

"Then Big Stan swung on him, but Marcus ducked and hit him in the nuts. I mean, I don't blame him. Big Stan is like six-three and two fifty. When he kneeled over from the pain, Marcus pulled him down and kneed him in the face. Big Stan fell backward and went out. Out of nowhere Troy punched Marcus in the face. Marcus didn't see it coming and staggered. I grabbed Troy and wrestled with him until he punched me in the face. I fell backward, and before I stumbled to the ground Marcus was on his ass," Stacy said proudly and full of excitement. She had been beat on many times over the years, but she had never had anyone who even considered defending her, not until her knight in shining armor came through.

Samara smiled without realizing it. Her little want-to-be-thug brother was trying to be a gentleman. And even better, Stacy risked injury to protect her brother instead of just letting it happen.

"As I got off the ground," Stacy continued, "Troy was stumbling toward it. Marcus was about to give him a nice beat down when I noticed Big Stan getting up. I yelled to Marcus, and he turned to see Big Stan getting up. Troy ran off, and people started to come out of the bowling center to see what was going on. I grabbed Marcus' arm and we hurried to the car and left."

Stacy took another deep breath before continuing.

"We were at a light on Benning Road when Stan's truck pulled up next to us. I told your brother to go. He looked over just as Troy pointed the gun out of the window and started firing as Marcus tried to speed off.

I don't know how many times they fired. I saw Marcus jerk and almost lose control of the car, so I knew he was hit." Stacy paused as the tears rolled down her eyes.

"It's OK, Stacy. I know my brother. He'll be just fine." After a pause Samara asked, "Do you know where he was hit?"

She pointed to the back of her left shoulder, then to her rib cage on the same side. "And he got shot in the leg somewhere."

"My brother is a warrior. He'll be just fine," Samara said. Stacy nodded.

About fifteen minutes later, Natalie and Jesse came into the waiting area. Samara gave her mother and brother a huge hug.

"How is he doing?" Natalie asked.

"I don't know yet. As far as I know, he's still in surgery," Samara said. Just after her statement a doctor came toward them.

"Who is Natalie Brown?" the doctor asked.

"I am," Samara's mother proclaimed.

"Hello, ma'am. My name is Dr. Stevenson. Your son is in stable condition. He was shot three times—once in the shoulder, once in the side, and once in the leg. The bullet in his side could have been fatal if it weren't for the car door slowing it down. He didn't suffer any serious injuries except for the loss of a lot of blood. Outside of that, he'll be fine."

Samara, Natalie, Jesse, and Stacy formed a group hug. All were very happy at the news. The doctor smiled and began to turn around. Natalie broke loose, went to the doctor, and gave him a big hug.

"Thank you, Dr. Stevenson. Thank you so much."

"It's no problem. I'm glad I was able to help."

Natalie nodded. "Can we see him?" she asked.

"You can see him, but he'll be out for a while."
Natalie nodded again and returned to her family.

Jesse was eyeing Stacy curiously. "Who are you?" he
asked.

Samara was about to answer, but Stacy beat her to it.
"Marcus's girlfriend."

The revelation came as a shock not only to Jesse and
Natalie, but to Samara as well. They all looked at each
other with looks of surprise on their faces.

"Hey, baby," Natalie said. "I'm sorry we have to meet
under these conditions, but I'm happy to meet you.
What's your name?"

"Stacy."

"It's a pleasure to meet you, Stacy. I guess we'll talk
a little later. The doctor said we can see MC, but he'll
be out for a while."

Natalie, Jesse, and Stacy began to walk toward the
room. Samara caught Stacy by the arm.

"We'll be right there," Samara said as Natalie and
Jesse continued down the hall. Samara whispered to
Stacy, "I need a thorough description of both of these
guys and where they hang out."

Chapter Nineteen

Murder, Murder

"Damn it!" Samara said to herself. No matter how hard she tried to avoid it, people kept tinkering with that switch. She wanted to be civilized, but people would rather turn on the killing machine. Her father had cursed her with the skills to eliminate opposition and rules that dictated when someone would face death. Threatening her life, or the lives of her immediate family or Tonya were grounds for termination.

Samara wanted to change the world without murder, the tool her father and grandfather had used in their attempts. She definitely didn't plan on killing black people. Her father had warned her that it would come to that, though.

"If you're going to change things you better start with the youth, the way I started teaching you when you were still impressionable," he told her. "Some of the older folks aren't up for change and they're going to get in your way and possibly threaten your life or the lives of the people you love. There'll be tough choices, and when they come your best option is to handle business the way I taught you."

Marcus didn't wake up until about seven that morning. He was greeted with hugs and kisses from the ladies and a heartfelt hug from his self-centered brother. Everyone was so excited that he was conscious and in good spirits.

"When were you going to introduce me to your girlfriend?" Natalie asked her son. Marcus looked over at Stacy, who was smiling.

"I was going to, Ma. Stacy, this is my mother. Ma, this is Stacy. See, now you've been introduced," Marcus said. They continued to converse, laugh, and joke for the next fifteen minutes.

"Hey, y'all, I gotta get some rest. Can y'all come and see me later?" Marcus asked. Everyone gave Marcus a big hug before exiting. Just as Samara hit the door, Marcus called to her. "Hey, sis, let me holla at you." She reentered and closed the door behind her. He stared her in the eyes.

"What?" Samara asked.

"No."

"No, what?"

"Maury, I'm your little brother and I know you better than anybody. I already know that you're going on a mission within the next two days and I'm telling you don't."

"Little brother, you must be under a lot of medication. You're telling me?"

"Maury, I'm asking you not to, for me, please."

"Why?"

"You have to wait until I get myself together so I can roll with you."

"Boy, please."

Marcus smiled. "For real, sis, ever since I started working at the center and seeing the difference we've made in those kids' lives, I know that we have something special going on. I mean, kids look up to me. They look forward to seeing me and playing games with me and listening to my advice. I mean these kids want to learn something more than rap songs and music videos. We've only been at it a few months and I already see that we're making a difference. Even the older kids my age are more positive. I know you're good at what you do, and those faggots deserve to get it, but we can't risk you getting locked up or hurt. Those children need you. I need you. There has to be another way."

Samara nodded. "I understand. I'll take it under advisement," Samara said as she went to kiss her brother on the forehead.

Marcus grabbed her shoulder and looked her squarely in the eyes.

"Samara, be careful," Marcus said as he released her and closed his eyes.

Later that evening, Samara sat on her bed slowly loading a magazine for one of her two Colt .40-caliber semi-automatic handguns. She was second-guessing whether she should go on the mission that she had already planned in detail. After her brother's words, along with her mother's before leaving the hospital, she was trying to decide whether it was really worth it.

The way Samara saw it there were only two ways to handle the situation. Stacy told the police the same story that she told Samara, so they had an accurate description of the suspects and the getaway vehicle. But even if the police were able to catch the suspects and muster a case strong enough to go to trial, Stacy and

Marcus would have to testify against them, which would make both of them targets for assassination until the trial, which could be up to a year away. At the same time, while the police were still looking for them, they might be looking for Marcus to finish the job, or Stacy to prevent her from testifying against them. Seeing as how leaving the situation in the police's hands could not assure Marcus's and Stacy's safety, that option became irrelevant. If she eliminated the threat quickly and discreetly, she wouldn't have to worry about all that.

Even still she considered Marcus's and her mother's words. She didn't want to disappoint her kids, her brother, or her mother. She also didn't want murder to become her only means of problem solving. That was the way the hoodlums in the streets handled theirs. Her mother had taught her better than that. She figured that after she dispatched the two who had attacked her brother, she would have to reevaluate how often she used her father's methods and not her mother's advice. The things her father taught her were for a different kind of mission than the one Samara had chosen, so she had to be a lot more judicious when implementing his rules and tactics.

Stacy had told Samara everything from Stan and Troy's real names and where they lived to the areas they frequented and the days and times they did. Finding them would not be a problem unless they thought the police were looking for them and they decided to flee town. The shooting had taken place a little more than eighteen hours ago, and the news had put out a vague description of the men and the car. Samara figured that wasn't enough for the men to flee town, so she was going to see them, and soon.

Just as Samara finished prepping her weapons, there was a knock at the door. She immediately retrieved her rifle from under the bed and rushed to the window. She surveyed the immediate area, including the street, the neighbor's windows, and the rooftops. The only thing she noticed that was different was Tonya's Toyota Camry parked across from her house. The knocking continued. She placed the rifle back under the bed, grabbed her two .40-caliber handguns, and headed downstairs.

Placing one gun in a shoulder holster, and pointing the other toward the door, she looked through the peephole. She noticed an agitated Tonya on the other side. She let her in and placed the other gun in the other holster on the opposite side of her chest.

Tonya walked through the door and shoved Samara so hard that she stumbled.

"What the fuck," Samara said, stunned by Tonya's actions.

"How in the hell is my little brother in the hospital fighting for his life and I know nothing about it? How is it that it happened more than twelve hours ago and my sister knows, but I don't? How is it possible that my little brother himself is the first to tell me?"

"Look, Tonya," Samara said. Tonya folded her arms across her chest, rolled her neck, and stuck out her lips, waiting for the explanation. "I was gonna tell you. I needed to clear my mind first. I was about to call you before I left out."

"You need those to clear your mind?" Tonya asked, pointing at Samara's guns.

"These aren't for my mind."

"They're to blow someone's mind out of their heads, right? Samara, I've known you all my life, but I'm starting to question how much I know you. I knew you had the potential and skills to be ruthless, but I didn't realize you had the heart. It's just like business as usual to you.

"When I found out that Smoke was murdered I figured it served him right with all the enemies he had and all the pain he had caused the community. I thought there was a very slight chance you had something to do with it, but now I know it was you and you alone who ended his life. Even now as I look into your eyes, I see the Samara I know, who is second-guessing whether she should be doing this. And at the same time, I see someone bent on revenge who already decided what she's gonna do. Samara—" Tonya attempted to continue before Samara interrupted her.

"Look, Tonya, I didn't want to have to expose you to this side of me. The reason I didn't tell you is because I didn't want you to try to talk me out of doing what I have to do. That's the reason my little brother told you, because he knows you and my mother are the only ones who can get me to reconsider. You can save those psychology lessons that we took together for someone else. Look, Tonya, I love you, but I have to get to work."

"Work? You consider committing murder, work?" Samara didn't answer her. "Look, Samara, I love Marcus like a brother and I think the bastards who did it ought to get it, but I don't think you should be the one dishing out the punishment." Samara ignored her and began gathering her belongings, including a wig, light windbreaker, and dark sunshades. "OK, give me a piece. I'm going with you," Tonya said finally. Samara stopped in her tracks.

"Are you sure?" Samara asked, and Tonya nodded. "OK. I'm gonna get you something small that I think you can handle. I'll be right back." Tonya nodded again, surprised that Samara had agreed so easily.

Samara headed into the basement, and a few seconds later Tonya heard a chime and the alarm saying, "Basement door open," followed by that door slamming shut. When Tonya ran to the back window on the first floor she saw Samara pulling off in an old Chevy Caprice that she hadn't seen Samara driving before.

Stacy told Samara that Stan basically lived at Troy's place. Troy was a small time local neighborhood drug dealer. If they weren't out partying together, they were at Troy's apartment smoking weed, drinking, and playing video games or having sexcapades with the neighborhood tramps. She told Samara that whenever they decided to lay low, they usually did so over Troy's. Troy lived in a huge apartment complex on a big, one-way circle called Paradise.

As Samara pulled around the huge circle, she passed a black Ford Expedition that she assumed belonged to Big Stan. It was parked on the left side of the street facing a lightly wooded area. She found a parking space about twenty feet away and left the car running. She went back to the truck and smashed the driver's side window. The truck's alarm went off. Samara opened the door. She ducked low and moved beside the car to the rear of the Stan's truck, outside of anyone's view.

Big Stan opened the apartment building's door and saw that his truck's alarm was the one that was going off.

"Hey, T, they fucking with my shit," he yelled before heading over to the truck to figure out what was going on. Troy soon exited the building with his gun in hand. As Big Stan approached the car, he could see the driver's side door was open. He figured some neighborhood kids had attempted to steal it or the nice stereo system inside, but were deterred by the truck's alarm system and The Club on the steering wheel. Before crossing the street he looked around to see if there were any kids running away from the scene and found none. Troy caught up with him.

After a car passed, and taking note of the blaring alarm on the truck, Troy and Big Stan crossed the street. Troy, who had grabbed Stan's keys when he grabbed his gun, hit the button on the keypad, killing the noisy alarm. Stan came around the front and Troy came from the rear. Big Stan was so concerned about his smashed window that he paid no attention to Samara, who was lying beside the car behind them in dark clothing. Samara heard car door slams and a car skid out as she got up to end the lives of her brother's assailants.

"Da fuck," Big Stan said, seeing a person in dark clothing rise from the ground. When Troy saw the fright on Big Stan's face, he turned to see what was wrong. Once he turned, raising his gun as he did, Samara took a shot. *Boom!* The single shot pierced Troy's skull and caused his body to slump to the ground. Blood and brain matter splattered on Big Stan, who was horrified by what had just happened. Samara hit him in his chest four times. He turned, took a couple of steps, and collapsed. She walked up to him, shot him in the head, and jogged toward the Caprice that she had driven over there.

"No!" Samara yelled. She was stunned to find that the car was gone. A few seconds had passed and she had to improvise. She had just murdered two people and knew the police would be coming soon. She had been relieved of her escape vehicle and the second half of her plan was in jeopardy. Samara ran back to the murder scene. *One of these assholes has to have the keys because they cut off the alarm remotely*, she thought.

After searching them both, she found the keys, hopped in the truck, and pulled off.

As she drove she knocked out the rest of the glass with a CD case in the truck and rolled down the passenger side window so it wouldn't be so obvious that she was driving a stolen vehicle. She drove the truck near the Deanwood Metro station, left it, and walked to the train station. Once she arrived, Samara avoided all cameras and the few passengers on the train at that time of night. She got on the train and remained incognito until she got off the bus that took her home.

Chapter Twenty

What Goes Around

Samara awoke the next morning with anxiety. It wasn't that she felt remorse for killing Big Stan and Troy, because she did not. Her nervousness came from the fact that her little plan nearly blew up, almost exposing her to injury, prison, or death. She realized that she was very fortunate to have gotten out of that situation, especially after being warned by her brother and her mother in so many words, not to do what they knew was on her mind at the time. She knew it was about time to start thinking more like her mother and less like her father.

She figured her mother must have prayed for her at some point, because that night could have been worse for her. What really made Samara feel bad was that her mother said she was going around doing the devil's bidding, and it was the absolute truth. Her mother and brother told her the truth, but she was so blinded with rage she couldn't hear it. Samara knew it was time she reexamined her life and her way of thinking.

She arrived at the center just before eight in the morning, a little more than an hour before it was set to open. She was surprised to see that Tonya's car was already there. She entered the center. Hearing the door open, Tonya came out in a workout outfit and headed toward the equipment lockers. Samara walked toward Tonya.

"Tonya," Samara called. Tonya glanced at her and continued toward the lockers. Samara met her at the lockers.

"Tonya, I'm sorry." Tonya reached into the locker, grabbed a set of headgear and gloves, and shoved them in Samara's chest. She then grabbed a second set for herself.

"Tonya? Girl, I'm sorry. I know I acted like an ass yesterday, and I'm sorry. I love you, Tonya, and I know that I violated our friendship last night. I know I should have listened to you, but I was too stubborn and selfish to do that last night. I'm going to do better, though. Look, I didn't even bring a gun today." Samara paused. "Please forgive me."

Tonya shoved Samara, causing the gloves and headgear to fall. Samara smiled. She went over and gave her best friend a huge hug. After a few seconds, Tonya returned the embrace.

"Samara, if you ever treat me like that again, I'm going to punch you in the face. You understand me?" Samara turned her loose.

"Whatever," she replied.

"OK. Try me," Tonya said, looking quite serious. Samara smiled.

"I wouldn't dare."

Tonya placed both sets of boxing equipment back inside the locker.

"Where's Stacy?" Tonya asked.

"She stayed with my mother yesterday. I guess she's at her house or at the hospital."

"Damn. It looks like she's in the family already. All she needs is a ring."

"You know what I'm saying," Samara agreed as they both laughed. "I really like Stacy. If she can keep her head on straight I would love for her to be my sister-in-law.

"I do, too. She is really sweet. She just had a tough upbringing, but I think she's gonna be special." Samara nodded in agreement.

They went and prepped the eating tables, pulling out the disposable Styrofoam bowls and dozens of small, one-serving boxes of brand name cereal. There were also plenty of packets of instant oatmeal if the children wanted hot cereal.

"I'm going to check out of here a little early today so I can spend some time with my brother," Samara said.

"That's cool. I'll go see him around lunch time, and when I come back, I'll just stay for the rest of the day."

"That sounds good."

The day went by pretty smoothly except for the kids who constantly asked where Marcus was. It was the second day he had missed, and the children weren't happy about it.

Tonya went to see Marcus and brought Stacy back with her. A few hours later Samara prepared to go and see her little brother. Stacy was adamant about going with Samara, even though Samara said she wanted to go alone. Stacy agreed that if Samara allowed her to go, she would stay in the waiting area while she talked with her brother.

As Stacy helped Donté and Tonya clean up, Samara made her way to the car to wait for Stacy. Samara was halfway to her car when she noticed three young women approach quickly, looking like they had something on their minds. She stopped and felt her purse for the gun that was not there.

"You put your hands on my uncle, bitch!" the tallest of the three said when the women were within fifteen feet of Samara.

Samara, seeing that the young women were poised to take action, and didn't look like she could talk them down, placed her left foot forward so that she would be ready to defend herself.

"I don't know what you're talking about," Samara responded.

"You will know what we're talking about when we beat that ass," the second young lady who was short and stout interjected.

"Look, I don't want no trouble," Samara said. She wasn't really concerned with the two who were talking. She was preoccupied with the one who wasn't. The silent one looked to be a few years older than Samara, and about business. She lagged about ten feet behind her associates.

The tall girl took a swing on Samara. Samara dodged the blow, grabbed her by the throat, and placed her right leg behind the young lady's leg. In one swift motion Samara used her leg to clip the young lady as she slammed her backward onto her head. The tall girl rolled on the ground, holding her head as the instant headache removed her from the action.

Just as Samara was turning to defend herself from the chubby one, the girl got a full head of steam and grabbed Samara's arms before she could rise from the choke/slam she had just performed. She grabbed Samara's arms, and with the momentum she fell on top of her. The fall knocked the wind out of Samara. The big girl released her grip and rose to hit Samara. After Samara's arms were free she tried to block the blow from the chubby young lady who sat on her. Samara was able to partially deflect the blow, but it still managed to make its way to her jaw.

Feeling the power of the blow that didn't even land flush certainly woke Samara up. She pulled on the young woman's shirt, causing her to lean over just enough so that Samara could get a straight jab through to the bridge of her nose. The girl finally rolled off of Samara.

Just as Samara was about to attempt to get up, she heard Stacy scream, "Maury!" The sharp and instant pain in her side was one like she had never felt before. She looked at her ribs and saw a knife protruding from her side with the third woman's hand extracting it and preparing to make a second attack. Samara rolled away, not quite believing how painful the stab was. As the blood began to flow, Samara's resolve to fight began to dissipate. She rose from the concrete.

The woman tried to stab Samara again, but Stacy caught her hand. Samara helped free the knife from the woman's hand, and Stacy began to punch the older woman in the face.

After hearing Stacy's initial scream before Samara got stabbed, Donté and Tonya had rushed outside. When Donté and Tonya got over to the action, they helped Stacy overpower the older lady and made sure the other two stayed down.

Samara began to feel light headed.

"Donté, help me get her in the car," Tonya said. Donté had just kicked the chubby one in the face for good measure and helped carry Samara to Tonya's car.

"I didn't plan on seeing my brother this way," Samara said before passing out.

Chapter Twenty-One

The Setup

Samara awoke feeling very groggy with an IV in her arm. Through bleary eyes she scanned her unfamiliar environment and was able to make out a few familiar faces. Marcus was sitting beside her, asleep in a wheelchair. Her mother was sitting in the chair across from her bed, also asleep. She tried to get up but a sudden rush of pain prevented her.

"Aghhh," she moaned, waking her mother and brother.

"Maury," her brother said. Natalie got up and came to her side.

"What in the hell happened?" Samara asked. Being heavily sedated, her mind was not sharp enough to recall the incident.

"You were in a fight with some girls. One of them stabbed you," her mother explained. Things began to become clearer for her. She remembered the fight and being stabbed. The last thing she remembered was Tonya, Donté, and Stacy helping her into a car.

"Who were they?" Samara asked.

"Stacy said they are associates of Joe," Marcus answered. Samara looked confused.

"Joe?" she asked.

"The one you manhandled in front of the center for messing with Stacy."

"Oh, Joe."

"You guys don't have to talk around me. I know who Joe is. Stacy told me all about herself, including that she used to work the streets and that Joe was her pimp." Both of her children looked surprised at first, but shrugged it off.

"Where's Stacy?"

"She went with Tonya and Donté to close the center for the day," Natalie responded. "They should be back any minute now."

"What about Jesse?" Samara asked. Marcus rolled his eyes.

"You mean the only child of mine that's in good health. I guess I'll be in here next, suffering from a heart attack," Natalie said. "It took me a while to get a hold of him, but he's on the way."

A few minutes later, Stacy, Donté, and Tonya entered the room. Tonya immediately went to give Samara a hug. Samara winced as she moved to lean forward. A hug from Stacy followed Tonya's hug . Donté stood just inside the door looking disgusted.

"How are you feeling?" Tonya asked.

Samara looked dumbfounded. "I hope that question was rhetorical."

Tonya smiled. "I was hoping to soften you up some. I know things seem bad now, but they just got worse."

"What now?"

"Well, when we went back to close the center, the

police were already inside looking around. They said it was part of the crime scene."

"And?"

"And they recovered drugs from inside the center."

"Drugs?" Samara asked in disbelief. "Did one of the kids have some weed on them or something?"

"Naw, they supposedly found a few ounces of crack and heroin. They were trying to insinuate that the center is a front for drug dealing," Tonya said.

"They planted that shit," Donté said, full of frustration.

"Tay," Samara called to him, "my mother's here, so watch the language."

"I'm sorry, Ms. Brown. I didn't mean any disrespect. I'm just frustrated that no matter how much good you do, somebody's always trying to hold you back."

"I understand, young brother," Natalie said. "And that's the devil who's trying to hold you back. It's OK for you to be angry. It'll make you want to beat them at their own game. They're attempting to outsmart y'all. They have a better playing hand than y'all, but if you use your brains and not violence"—she looked over at Samara—"you will overcome."

"Did anyone see when or where they recovered the drugs from?" Samara asked.

"No. Everyone was outside trying to see about you when they were inside."

"Well who are they going to put the drugs on?"

"You!" Tonya said emphatically. "They're saying you're the ring leader and the attack was gang related. I'm sure they're going to send some detectives over here to harass you."

Samara shook her head in disbelief. They had her. Even though all of the information and evidence was a fabrication of the truth, it was a very convincing one.

Natalie leaned over to her daughter's ear.

"Violence rarely solves problems. It usually causes more. Intelligence is the only proven problem-solver, and it's about time you used some."

She rose from Samara's side.

"Do y'all see what is going on?" Natalie asked, looking around the room. Everyone's face was blank.

"Think about it. The center has been able to change in a matter of months what the city hasn't been able to change yet. It's run by a young black woman without any help from the government or any private for or non-profit corporations. And just a couple of weeks ago, Samara had a run-in with two white women who were looking to impose their will on the center. How does it look if a young black woman formed a model that countless politicians and strategists have yet to figure out how to do?

"Although the Black Panthers had good qualities and bad, the good they did was never the focus of the media. That's because there are still many who want to see the majority of black people held in check by the system, the system I've been telling my children about since they could walk. If the center is a success and that success spreads to other cities and people of color start to rise up and make a better life for themselves, it would be displeasing to the system and the power structure that's charged with maintaining it. It's up to you to make sure that y'all succeed and deal some blows to the system. As y'all can see, it's not going to be easy."

"That's deep, Ms. Brown," Donté said.

"That isn't the half of it, but it's an adequate warning. Samara knows what's going on and what you all have to do." There was silence for the space of a minute while they pondered her words.

"Thank you for saving me, Stacy," Samara said. Stacy, who was standing near Donté, nodded.

"I was only returning the favor. You saved me twice. I still owe you one. Oh, yeah, the girl who stabbed you might be joining you here. She caught a serious beat down." Everyone laughed.

"Tonya, what about the video recordings from inside the center?" Samara asked.

"They got the copies," Tonya answered. Samara was visibly upset. "But I know some tricks, too. We'll be alright."

"I hope so," Samara said.

About a half hour later two detectives entered the hospital room and greeted everyone. No one acknowledged them.

"Listen," the average sized black male detective said to everyone. "My name is Detective Kearney. This is Detective Sellers," he said, pointing to the taller black man. "I need to speak with Ms. Brown alone, and Detective Sellers needs to speak with each of you separately."

Natalie was incensed.

"My daughter is in here trying to recuperate from a violent attack that happened only a few hours ago, and now you want to question her—alone?"

"It's OK, Ma. I got this," Samara responded. Detective Kearney was obviously relieved to avoid the confrontation and be able to actually question Samara alone.

"It'll only be a few minutes," the detective reassured Natalie. She rolled her eyes and continued out the door. Everyone filed out behind her.

"Ma'am, I need to talk with you, too," Detective Sellers yelled to Natalie as he exited. "Ma'am?" She ignored him. He shook his head and closed the door behind him.

Detective Kearney stared at Samara for a moment. She was so attractive. Although she was ten years his junior, according to his info, that number meant nothing to him. But his boss had sent him on a mission, so he would have to save the flirting for another day.

"How are you feeling, Ms. Brown?"

"Get to what you came here for," she said, abruptly cutting off any small talk.

"OK. Well, first off, who were the girls who attacked you?"

Samara contorted her face. "The hell if I know. I never saw them a day in my life until this afternoon. I mean, you're the detective. Why don't you tell me?"

"I have their names, but I need to know what prompted them to attack you," the detective responded.

"Did you try asking them?" Samara asked.

"I did. What they told me was that the attack stemmed from a drug deal during which they received a bad quality product."

Samara wore a look of confusion. "Detective, what exactly are you saying?"

"You asked if I did my job," the detective said, returning the sarcasm dealt out by Samara. "I told you what was said when I did my job."

"They come to my center and attack me, then accuse me of dealing drugs, and you believe that?"

"I'm a detective. I gather all of the evidence and go whichever way it leads. That's why I'm here questioning you so that I can gather all the evidence before I begin to accuse and arrest."

"In that case, I'll make it easy for you. I never used, possessed, or sold any drugs in my life. I run a center to keep the youth from getting involved in that type of stuff. I run outreach programs to help adults who're caught up with drugs and alcohol, so they can get their lives together. What they told you was worse than a lie. It's slander and defamation." The detective nodded.

"Yeah, I understand all that, but some officers found a nice little package of crack and dope in the center." Samara began to lose her composure.

"What the hell you mean you found dope in my center? Who found dope in my center?"

"Some officers who were working the scene."

"What scene? I got stabbed outside, nearly twenty feet away from the center. How does the center become part of a crime scene? And more importantly, who saw the officers retrieve drugs from the center?" Samara asked, casting a serious look of suspicion the policeman's way.

"Look, when they got there you were gone, so they had probable cause to search for any other victims or assailants."

"Without a warrant?" The detective looked Samara over suspiciously.

"You seem pretty concerned with the legality of the search rather than what the search uncovered. It makes me wonder if you already knew what was in there, and now you're looking for a way to have that evidence tossed out." Samara pursed her lips.

"To the contrary, detective, I have a problem with officers planting evidence in my center and accusing law-abiding citizens of committing crimes when they are just trying to make a positive difference in the community."

"I'm done with the questioning for now, but unless you're gonna tell me who the drugs belong to, we're going to charge you with conspiracy, obstruction, and maybe even possession. Do you understand?"

"Yeah, I understand. I understand that you're full of shit. If you wanna know who the drugs belong to, find out the name of the officer who found it and you'll have your answer. And you can charge me with whatever you want. I don't give a damn. I'll see you in court with those frivolous charges.

"You seem like a halfway intelligent brother, but if you can't see that your massah done sent you down here to put the press on this fair-skinned, uppity nigga girl who's stirring up trouble by trying to help her people without his consent, then you're really not that intelligent at all. What your massah don't understand is that I'm on a mission and it's going to take a lot more than what he's put together so far to derail it. So you run tell your massah that I'm here to stay and my ass is here to kiss."

The detective was both disgusted and amazed at Samara's little speech. He was amazed at how intelligent she was in addition to her beauty. But he was disgusted at being called an errand boy or spy who betrayed his people. He realized that the situation with the drugs in the center seemed shady at best. The statements that were coerced from Samara's attackers in turn for consideration of lesser charges meant that somebody wanted her very badly. But one of his superiors who had looked out for him many times before had told him to make the case happen. So he was just doing his job.

"Don't leave town," the detective said.

Samara simply shook her head in disappointment.

Chapter Twenty-Two

The Eyes of a Killer

The next morning Samara lay in her hospital bed watching the news. When the segment concerning her and the center came on, she turned up the volume. In the corner of the screen was a picture of Samara with her name under it.

"This hour we have more information on the attack of Samara Brown, the charismatic community leader of Ward 4. Last night we broke news that Ms. Brown was stabbed in front of the community center that she owns and operates. Today there are allegations that the attack may have been drug related. A subsequent search of the center uncovered a large amount of crack cocaine and heroine." Samara's stomach dropped when she heard the report. She suddenly felt nauseous.

The reporter continued.

"There has been speculation that community center is a front for gang members to sell drugs. Since the center opened in late May, there have been two shootings and one stabbing. One of those shootings took place inside the center. So far five people have been killed and

four others, including Samara and a seven-year-old
boy have been wounded by violence in or directly in
front of the Future Leaders Community Center.

"The councilman for Ward 4 had this to say about
the attack and the drugs being recovered."

A prerecorded clip of the councilman appeared on
the screen.

"For this center to have children around so much violence is unacceptable. The worst part about it is that
not only are the children placed in harm's way by
being at the center, but it looks like they're dealing
drugs right in front of them. They have gang wars taking place inside and outside of the building. The center is run by private funds, obviously to keep away the
scrutiny of where the money comes from away from
the government. Not only is that rare when dealing
with a non-profit corporation, it's the MO of organized
crime.

"I'm in the process of sponsoring an emergency
meeting to have the center closed indefinitely. And I
will bring charges against and prosecute anyone involved in illegal activity at the center to the fullest ex-
tent of the law."

The reporter came back on and switched to a different story.

"Damn it!" Samara said. They were making things
more and more difficult with the negative public rela-
tions campaign. *People are going to judge me just by
that asshole's comments*, Samara thought. It was OK,
though. Samara had heard him slip a couple of times,
enough that it no longer sounded like he was giving an
opinion, but it easily bordered on slander.

Then something suddenly dawned on Samara. She
wondered why the councilman had spoken so badly of
the center, and so suddenly. He hadn't even let the po-

lice really begin their investigation before he put all of that biased information out there. What happened with innocent until proven guilty? The councilman had an angle on the situation, and she needed to figure out exactly what it was.

Things were looking very bad for Samara and the center. The emergency meeting that the councilman planned to hold could take place within a few days. She was sure the police would prohibit her from reopening for at least another day or two as they went through every inch of the center, including confidential employee, financial, and participant records. Now that the operation had been labeled a front for drug dealing, it would also be investigated for money laundering and other multi-jurisdictional crimes. It was going to take a lot for the center to rebound.

"Oh shit!" Samara uttered. She had been labeled as a member of an ongoing criminal enterprise. It was very likely they were going to search her house. If they found the arsenal that she had in there, they would definitely associate her with drugs or preparing for a small war. She had to get home and secure her weapons.

Samara got out of the bed. There was still that nagging pain in her side, but the biggest problem was the dizziness of the drugs and not being mobile for twelve hours. She took a seat in the chair in front of the bed and the phone rang. Samara was hesitant at first, but answered on the fourth ring.

"Hello."

"Hey, Maury."

"Hey, girl. You're just who I wanted to talk to."

"Maury, I'm here. Call me back," Tonya said. Samara smiled.

"OK," she said and hung up. Tonya had used a code

Samara had inadvertently taught her. Whenever Samara had something of importance to talk with Tonya
about she would tell her to call her back, which meant
from a more secure line or away from certain people.
"I'm here" meant that Tonya was already where
Samara needed her to be.

Samara picked up her plastic container of water and
poured it directly into the receiver of her phone. She
did that in case one of the nurses asked where she was
going. Then she got up and walked out of the room.
Samara was caught off guard by a police officer sitting
on post beside her door.

"Hold on, ma'am. Where are you going?" the officer
asked.

"Who are you?"

"I'm Officer Sans. I'm here to make sure you're not
attacked again."

Samara didn't really believe him, but she also didn't
care so long as he didn't get in her way.

"I didn't request any protection."

"I'm just following orders," the officer replied.

"Whatever. My phone is dead. I'm going to use the
phone. May I use the phone, officer?"

"What's all that for? I don't care what you do. Just
don't go too far."

"Or what?" Samara asked, becoming irritated.

"Just don't do it," the officer said, and then he
turned his attention away from her.

"Yeah, whatever," she responded. The officer ignored
her. Samara walked around the corner and entered an
unlocked and empty observation room. She dialed a
nine before dialing her home phone number.

"Maury," Tonya answered.

"Yes."

"Have you seen the news?"

"I have. It's ugly." There was a brief pause. "Since you're there, you already know what I need you to do."

"All I need to know is where."

Samara told her in slang and misdirection where all of her weapons and ammunition were stored.

"You be careful, and hurry up," Samara said. "They're trying hard to take us down, so please be careful. I'm about to go check on my brother."

"Maury, he was released last night. He came to see you before he left, but we couldn't wake you."

"OK. I think that I'm going to be discharged today. We have to prepare a little press conference to stave off some of this negative press. I'll talk to you later."

"OK. I got a present for you, too," Tonya said as she hung up the phone.

The next day Samara was home resting in her bed when the doorbell rang. She had never felt more uncomfortable in her own house than she did at that moment. There was not a single gun in the house, save for a stun gun. Tonya and Stacy had removed all of the weapons just in time. Within a few hours of Tonya and Samara's conversation the police came through and ransacked the place.

The doorbell rang again. She went and peeped through the window. There weren't any strange cars or anything out of place. The only way she could see who was at the door was to open the window or go downstairs. The window opened and she stuck her head out. It was Donté.

She slowly moved down the stairs, still feeling the pain from the stitches in her side. She went to the door and opened it. They hugged each other and she allowed him to enter.

"How are you feeling?" Donté asked.

"I'm about eighty percent, but a lot better than yesterday."

"That's good. I saw your little brother yesterday. He's doing better too."

"How's J-Rock doing?"

"He's doing a lot better. He's still going through therapy and stuff, though. It's funny you asked. The day you got stabbed, he was trying to find out who was responsible so he could go on a mission," Donté said and they both laughed. "I told him don't worry about it. I already got that covered," Donté continued with a wicked grin.

Samara stared in his eyes. She did not like what she saw in them.

"Donté?" she questioned. He looked away. "Donté, did you—" Donté interrupted her.

"You're a good judge of people and body language. Don't ask a question you already know the answer to."

Samara was mad at herself. She already knew that Donté was capable of murder, but she hadn't had a chance to talk him down from going after Joe. When she had looked him in the face while she lay in the hospital bed, she saw rage in his eyes, the kind of anger that clouded judgment and took lives.

"I understand you were trying to look out for me, but you can't go around killing people," Samara pleaded.

Donté looked at her like she was crazy. He couldn't believe what he heard. Samara knew where he was going before he began to respond.

"Well you're my boss and the leader at the center. I'm just following your example." Samara shook her head.

"Have they found his body yet?" she asked, ignoring his comment.

"I don't think so."

"Donté, I really need you out here. Killing folks leads to life sentences and being killed. I see in you a very strong leader, but you're gonna have to grow up fast and put behind you that aggressive mentality to kill anyone who causes you friction. I know I've done that a few times, but I was raised by parents with two totally different points of view.

"My daddy killed people. He taught me how to kill people. He taught me that if someone tried to murder me or my family it was up to me to make sure they didn't get a second chance. My mother taught me to use my head. I'm telling you this because she's already rebuked me twice for becoming a murderer instead of an intelligent leader. She taught me how to win battles by outthinking my enemies instead of overpowering. I'll be perfect when I can combine what both of them taught me. But I've known for a long time that to keep on killing folks won't solve problems. There's just been a lot of temptation lately."

"I know what you mean. There's been more beef since the center opened than there was since the beginning of the year. You talk a lot like my brother. He's always trying to talk some sense into me like you are. He uses that word temptation a lot, too. He's always talking about me going to church and getting my mind right with God. After killing Joe, I think I'm going to take him up on that and go to church tomorrow."

"That's good. I'm going with you because my mother keeps preaching the same thing to me. I can't wait to meet your brother," Samara said with a huge smile.

"I can't wait for you to meet him, too. It won't be long now. But until then he told me he was very proud of what you're doing at the center and he looks forward to meeting you too. He'll be coming home soon," Donté said and Samara nodded. "So what's up with the drugs they planted at the center?" Donté asked.

"It's cool. Tonya got a recording from the cameras showing two officers planting the drugs and pretending that they miraculously found them. They think they got us, but we got them by the balls. Not only is someone getting fired for this, somebody's going to jail," Samara said, and Donté laughed.

"Why didn't they search for the cameras or the video?"

"Did you know that we had cameras in the center?" He shook his head, indicating that he did not, so Samara continued. "Tonya ordered the system when she ordered the door entry system. It just took longer to install the hidden cameras. There are no monitors or visible recording system. A version is recorded to the hard drive of one of the computers in the computer lab and another is broadcast over the Internet directly to my and Tonya's home computers. If nothing happens that day, we delete it."

"I guess that was right on time, huh?"

"Was it! If Smoke wouldn't have been so brazen and forced us to upgrade our security, we would lose the center and possibly be going to jail."

"So when are you going to give it to the media?"

"I'm going to wait and see how far the Council is going to carry this. I think that shady-ass councilman that was at the opening day celebration when the police were harassing you and J-Rock is up to no good," Samara explained.

"I think so too. He was talking real bad about us. Usually those politicians say their little piece and wait until the police have done some serious investigating before they start talking like that. He was talking like he already knows we're guilty and he's going to ready the noose, and all they have is planted evidence. They don't even have a suspect yet, but he accuses all of us of being guilty. He knows something. He's probably in cahoots with those crooked cops who put the drugs there in the first place."

"It's cool. By holding on to that evidence until the meeting, it'll do more damage to him and probably smoke out his accomplices. He's got friends in the department for sure." Samara paused. "I need a video camera," Samara said suddenly.

"Why?" Donté asked.

"So I can record the councilman's expression when he sees that video."

Chapter Twenty-Three

Fallen

The next day, Samara, Tonya, Donté, Stacy, and Marcus found themselves in church with Natalie. None of them had been there for a while, and some not since childhood. It was a beautiful service that all of them enjoyed. Donté, Stacy, and Marcus joined the church. Tonya was already a member, although her attendance was erratic. Samara wanted to rejoin, but she had to work out some wrinkles in her life and way of thinking before she could commit herself wholly to the church and the Lord. Natalie told her that sounded like an excuse.

They went to have breakfast at the International House of Pancakes in Arlington, Virginia. Stacy and Marcus were never a foot apart after getting out of the car. Samara and Tonya continually laughed at them. Donté walked up and grabbed Tonya's hand as if they were a couple. Tonya looked at him, half smiling and half surprised. Donté looked back at Stacy and Marcus. Everyone looked back at the new couple holding hands just the way Donté had grabbed Tonya's hand, trying to mock them. They all laughed at the scene. After a ten-minute wait, they were seated.

"Have they set a date for the hearing?" Natalie asked.

"Yes. My lawyer called me the other night and said that the hearing is going to take place in a week," Samara responded.

"What happens to the center until then?"

"Well, the police chief under some legislation passed a couple of years ago has the power to close it down for up to four days. That's expired. Only the city council has the power to close it on an emergency basis until the hearing. So, we're going to open the place for business tomorrow and see how they want to carry the situation."

"I think we should set up a little press conference just in case they decide to shut us down, so we can tell our side of the situation," Tonya said.

"I think we should open the center and have a press conference," Donté agreed. Natalie looked at her son for his opinion.

"I'm with my sisters," Marcus said.

Everyone's attention then turned to Stacy.

"I'm with my man," Stacy said. Everyone laughed. "Seriously, whatever it takes to get the center back open for good, I'm for."

"Agreed," Samara replied. "Ma?"

"Yes?"

"I was thinking about naming the center after Dad." Everyone remained silent. It was a sensitive area for Samara and her brother, but much more for Samara, who had spent more time with her father than either of her brothers. Natalie smiled.

"I think it's a good idea. He was a good man at heart. It was just his methods I didn't approve of. He helped to make you who you are and made the center a reality in so doing. He wanted something different for you, but once he saw your vision he put his aside and supported you. I think it's a great idea. What do you think, MC?"

Marcus smiled and nodded. "It's a good idea. My father would have been proud to see me do some good in my life instead of running the streets. I've always been proud of him. I just took a wrong turn when he stopped coming around so much. I would be very proud to have my father's name on top of the center," Marcus said with tears glistening in his eyes. It caused his sister's eyes to become teary along with the rest of the females at the table. Donté nodded. Stacy kissed Marcus on the cheek.

Natalie took a tissue from her purse and dabbed at her eyes.

"Well, I guess it's unanimous," she said.

The waitress came over and took everyone's orders. At that moment two familiar faces entered the dining area. Ms. Simms and Ms. Russell, the white ladies from the July Fourth water balloon fight at the center, entered with an older white man wearing a black suit with a gun on his waist who looked like a detective or agent of some sort. Samara watched as the hostess escorted them to their table. Samara and Ms. Simms stared at each other. Ms. Simms smiled, got up from her seat, and headed over to Samara's table.

"Hello, everyone," Ms. Simms greeted. "May I speak with you a moment, Ms. Brown?"

Tonya looked concerned when she recognized the woman. "Hey, aren't you the lady that tried to stop our water fight?" she asked.

Samara stood and held up her hand. "Tonya, I got it," Samara said. Samara and Ms. Simms exited the building together.

"Look, Samara, I'm sorry we got off to a bad start," Ms. Simms said once they were outside. "I'm also very sorry to hear that you were attacked," Ms. Simms said.

"Look here, Marsha, you don't have to bullshit me. I've looked in your eyes. I know you don't mean what you said, so tell me what you really have on your mind."

"I resent that. I am sorry that you got attacked. Samara, I told you that all I wanted to do was help you, but you wanted to do it the hard way. Now look. They're about to close your little center down and guess where Change for Urban America's new DC headquarters is going to be located? And we appreciate you putting all of your money into fixing up the center for us. The city is going to pay us to stay there, whereas it costs you so much just to be there. We'll hold a staff position for you, though," Ms. Simms said and smiled. She was so pleased with herself.

"If I thought they were going to take my center to give to you, I would burn it to the ground," Samara said through clenched teeth.

"Good. I'll be sure to share that information with the police real soon."

"You think you've won, don't you?"

"I know I have," Ms. Simms said matter-of-factly. "If you had done any thinking previously and accepted my offer, you wouldn't have to go through with all of this. Let me tell you what your problem is." Samara was amazed.

"My problem? I'm staring at my problem. And if I weren't a lady and acted like a bitch like you, I would solve my problem with this," Samara said and raised her fist. "But I'm better than that."

"Please. I hope you're not trying to convince me of

that. Anyway, let me tell you what your problem is. The problem is that you're racist," Ms. Simms said to Samara's astonishment. "You think that if a white person wants to help, then there must be an ulterior motive. If you would have just taken the help which you obviously needed, then everyone's life would have been a little easier."

"I'm racist? This cannot be coming from the person who labeled blacks as 'you people.' Let me tell you what your problem is. You're ignorant. You think that blacks can't accomplish anything on their own, especially not without the checks and balances that the white people establish. Some little college educated colored girl couldn't have established a more effective model than the one you and your organization have worked on for years. You're the racist, and although you may be able to hide it from some, it's plainly obvious to me. I wish that councilman you have in your pocket could see that," Samara said, testing her. She was looking for a sign that Ms. Simms and the councilman were working together. If they were allied, it would be great leverage for Samara.

Ms. Simms gasped and remained silent for a few seconds, then she smiled.

"I wish you luck in trying to prove that. This is what I'll do for you, though. While you're in jail, I'll send you some pictures of the changes we make to the center and have the kids write you."

Samara smiled. "The only time I'll be in jail is to visit you and let you know that you're not as smart as you think."

"We'll just have to see about that," Ms. Simms said with a frown.

"That we will. That we will."

* * *

The next morning Samara, Tonya, Stacy, Marcus, Donté, and J-Rock were at the center bright and early, preparing to open it for the day. After making breakfast, they got the daily tasks and events together.

About ten minutes before the center was set to open there was a knock at the door. Stacy was the closest to the door, so she walked over to see who it was.

"It's two police officers," Stacy said.

Samara and Tonya headed straight to the door. On the other side of the door they found Officer Presto and her partner.

"This facility is closed down," Officer Presto yelled through the door. "What are y'all doing in there?"

"About to open," Samara responded.

"Under whose authority?" the officer asked.

"Look, sister, I know you're not the brightest, so let me break it down for you," Samara said to both officers' surprise. "The police department can only close the center for four days at best. It's been nearly a week. Unless the council holds an emergency session and declares that we are to stay closed until the hearing, we'll be here."

"You know, you got a real smart mouth. You better watch it. One day you might find a fist in it," Officer Presto said with a devious smile.

"I know you didn't just go there," Tonya interjected.

"Are you threatening me?" Samara asked the officer.

Officer Presto looked at her partner before turning her attention back to Samara.

"I wouldn't call it a threat. It's more like a warning mixed with a promise," Presto responded. Her partner giggled.

"That's cool. I already told you to come see me on your day off. We have a boxing ring and equipment in here. Come see me."

The officer was infuriated at Samara's boldness. "I'll be there, real soon."

"Just let me know when and come on through. I'll take care of everything else."

The officer's partner shook his head. They walked back to their cruiser and began talking into their walkie-talkies. Just after nine o'clock Samara opened the doors to the center. A few kids saw Samara open the center and rushed inside. The two officers followed the children inside and stood post just inside the door. Tonya went to meet them.

"Is there a problem, officers?" Tonya asked.

"If you want there to be one," Officer Presto responded. Samara came over to them.

"What's the matter now, officer? This is bordering on harassment."

"I have orders from my lieutenant to remain here until he arrives. Do you have any other questions?" Officer Presto asked. Samara and Tonya walked away without responding.

About an hour later with the center in full swing with children and young adults learning and having fun again, the uninvited guests began to pour in. It began with the chief of police and his subordinates, and ended with the councilman and a host of media. All of the officers and the politician observed the children. They attempted to interact with them for the media's sake, but the staff and children seemed too busy for them. Samara pulled Tonya by the arm into her office. Samara smiled at Tonya.

"What?" Tonya asked.

"Watch this," Samara said. She picked up the phone and dialed a number. Tonya had a curious expression on her face.

"May I speak with the mayor, please?" She paused. "Samara Brown . . . OK. Hey, Mr. Mayor, how are you? . . . I'm OK. I was wondering if you were running for a second term? Oh, I was just asking because your boy the councilman thinks he runs the city already. He's down here with the chief and the media saying it's up to him to clean up the mess you made by endorsing me as a community leader." Samara hung up the phone.

"What happened?" Tonya asked anxiously.

"He said he's on his way and slammed the phone in my ear. He's heated."

Samara and Tonya left her office. A few minutes later the councilman pulled her aside.

"Look, I know you've been through a lot in the last week or so, but I need you to close this place down until we have a hearing on its future," the councilman said.

"I thought our future had already been decided as far as you were concerned," Samara responded.

"Things aren't looking good for you or the center to be truthful with you, but everyone is afforded due process."

Samara stared at him. "Due process? What do you know about that? Is due process the reason you went on TV and proclaimed us guilty before the police could finish their investigation? The reason the media used the word *alleged* is to protect themselves from slander and libel suits? I didn't once hear you say anything except that we were responsible and you were going to get us." She paused for effect. "Sounds like a good lawsuit to me."

He smiled. "Thanks for the heads up. Now that the

media is here, I'll be sure to recant those words. I don't need words with all the evidence that we got. Now go ahead and close this thing down until the hearing and save me the time of going downtown and forcing the closure."

"What do you have against me and this center?"

"It's nothing personal."

"Just taking care of business, huh?" Samara asked. The councilman smiled and nodded. "Well I'm going to suggest that you and Ms. Simms rethink y'all's business plan." The councilman was instantly on edge, nervous, and shifty. Samara received the visual confirmation that they were in it together.

"I don't know what you're talking about," he responded.

"Well I guess you're going to do what you have to do, because I'm not closing this place down for one minute."

"We'll see about that."

Samara nodded in agreement. She noticed the mayor entering, but the councilman did not, having his back turned toward the door.

"Who, me?" Samara asked, pointing to herself, acting as if the mayor was gesturing to speak with her. "Oh, the mayor wants to speak with you," Samara said to the councilman. He turned around and walked over to the visibly upset mayor. Samara headed for Tonya.

"What did you say to him?" Tonya asked, smiling at Samara.

"That he better stop playing with me." They both laughed. A few minutes later the councilman walked over to Samara.

"You got a week's reprieve. The day the hearing takes place will be the last day of the center as you know it. I wish you luck on your legal troubles."

"Certainly. I wish you luck with yours," Samara said, smiling.

"What are you talking about?" a confused councilman asked.

"Have a good day, councilman," Samara said politely. The councilman frowned and left the building.

The rest of the day went very well for Samara. The reopening of the center brought a joy back into her life that she had desperately missed. She scored a preliminary victory against the councilman and his bid to do her and the center in. Things could not have been better until she received a call close to midnight.

"Hello," Samara answered, still half asleep. She heard a male crying on the other end. "Hello," she said again, trying to get a response from the caller.

"They got Tay," the voice said.

"Who is this?"

"J-Rock. They killed Donté."

"What! No! It can't be Donté," Samara said as tears filled her eyes. J-Rock continued to sob.

"They killed my man. They killed my man. These motherfuckers going pay. Tay, what did they do?"

"Where is he, J-Rock?"

"He's heading to the medical examiner's office."

Samara hung up the phone and burst into tears.

Chapter Twenty-Four

Introducing Michael McMillan

Samara had been very ill the last couple of days. She was both nauseated and frustrated. She couldn't believe that things could change so much in two weeks. In that time frame things went from good, to bad, to ugly.

Just a few weeks ago everyone was laughing, joking, and playing. Since then things had changed dramatically. She was facing the permanent closing of the center. That meant the young folks would be back on the streets and into foolishness. She was recuperating from being stabbed, and under investigation for various violations of the law as a result of the attack. Most importantly, her dear friend and apprentice had been murdered, and she had no idea who had committed the offense. Her situation was beyond ugly.

She had to prepare herself that day to bury her buddy Donté. She had seen him grow from a hoodlum who cursed her out, to one of the finest leaders the center had. Donté was special. He always had the potential to be a leader, but he got sidetracked when his big brother and mentor had to do a stretch.

Samara was a step ahead of her other problems. She had the video to combat the closing. She had healed well from the stabbing, and all that remained was a small scar on an otherwise flawless body. The greatest problem, though, the death of her lieutenant, was the one she couldn't do anything about.

The funeral home was filled beyond capacity. Samara, Tonya, Stacy, Marcus, Natalie, Jesse, and J-Rock got there about a half hour before the wake. On the front row Samara saw Donté's sobbing mother, along with his little sisters and other family members. There was a gentleman Samara did not recognize who was consoling the mother. He was about six feet tall, muscular, and very handsome. He looked to be in his late twenties.

They all proceeded in a line to see their fallen friend. Tonya, Stacy, and Natalie broke down into tears when they got to the casket. Samara, J-Rock, and Marcus tried hard to choke back their tears. There was plenty of weeping throughout the place.

Samara went to say her condolences to Donté's mother.

"I'm so sorry for your loss," Samara said, grabbing the grieving mother's hand. "I loved Donté like a brother. The kids loved him, too. He was a good young man and he's really going to be missed." Donté's mother managed a smile through her tear-stained face. The man beside her also smiled.

"How are you doing, Ms. Brown?" the man asked. Samara looked confused at this man knowing her name. "I'm Mike, Donté's big brother," he explained. "I'm sorry that we had to meet like this."

Samara smiled and gave him a hug. "I don't know what happened. He was doing so good." She felt the need to somehow explain what went wrong to the man who had inadvertently left her in charge of his brother.

"It's going be all right. Can I speak with you when the services are over?" Mike asked. She nodded and walked away.

The service went as well as could be expected for the passing of a loved one. A lot of people had many good things to say about Donté. The most consistent thing that was said was about his transformation over the last couple of months into a very responsible and good young man.

At the repast Mike caught up with Samara.

"Hello again, Ms. Brown."

She smiled. "My name is Samara." She pointed to her mother. "Ms. Brown is my mother." They enjoyed a light laugh.

"I was really looking forward to meeting you, but it's unfortunate that we had to meet like this. Tay had nothing but good things to say about you. At one point I thought you were going to replace me. You were very special to him. Everything you told him he took to heart." As Mike spoke tears welled up in Samara's eyes. "He loved you like a big sister."

"I loved him, too."

"Now, he told me you were beautiful and sexy, and he put emphasis on both, but I couldn't really conceptualize until right now. Samara, you are one of the most beautiful females I've ever seen. Plus you're smart and have a conviction to help our people and the youth especially. Samara, you're perfect."

Samara began to blush. She really appreciated the compliments, and noticed that he was kind of flirting with her. Apparently his attraction for her was instantaneous. And when she saw him for the first time she was already head over heels for him. The only problem she had with him thus far was the fact that he had been incarcerated. What he was arrested for might make a big difference in whether she would bother with him.

"He told me you were locked up, but you might be released soon." Mike nodded. "Are you out, or did they just let you out to come to his funeral?"

"I'm free, so to speak. I could have gotten out six months ago, but I would have to do that time on papers which was unacceptable. I just stayed so that once they let me out I wouldn't have The Man forcing me to piss in a cup and come see him once a week, looking for a reason to send me back. I got out five days ago, the day after he was killed."

"What were you in for?" Samara asked.

"Selling a lot of dope." Samara immediately frowned. Mike laughed at her sudden change of expression. "I'm just kidding, girl. Tay told me that you were concerned about why I was in, but that he wouldn't tell you why. You were looking so serious, I couldn't pass that up." Samara managed to laugh it off.

"I saw an officer manhandling my little brother," Mike continued, "so I had something to say about it. He attempted to manhandle me. He caught the worse end of that altercation, but when they got together they got the upper hand. I got three years for assaulting a police officer. The only reason I didn't get more time was because I had witnesses who said I was trying to defend myself," Mike said.

Samara breathed a sigh of relief.

"That's horrible," she responded

"Yeah, it was unfortunate. My brother started messing up after I went in. And the police began to harass him even more. He only started to come around after you came into his life. I am very thankful for that."

"It was a pleasure working with him. He was my right-hand man."

"Is it true that you offered him up?" Mike asked, laughing.

"It wasn't like that. I just wanted a little respect that I hadn't received thus far. I figured that I would earn it or take it, but I was going to have it. We weren't going to have a fist fight. I had a boxing ring and gloves in the center. I just told him we could break it in."

Mike laughed hard. Other people looked over at Mike and wondered what was so funny at such a somber event. He quieted down.

"You're crazy. He told me that he saw you put in work, though, and he was glad he didn't get in that ring." Samara burst into laughter, and Mike continued. "I've talked to just about everyone and no one knows what happened. I keep hearing that it might have been retaliation for killing some guy named Smoke, but no one knows for sure." Samara felt butterflies forming in her stomach. She could not believe it. She was hoping her misdeed hadn't cost her buddy his life. The slightly worried look she wore was easily picked up by Mike.

"We'll talk about it later. This isn't the time or place," Mike said as Samara nodded in agreement. "We need to have a long conversation anyway."

"About what?"

"You."

"What about me?"

"Me and you," Mike said confidently.

Samara eyes bulged and her mouth gaped open. "What about me and you?"

"You still mess with that chump?" Mike asked with a grin.

"Who is that?" Samara asked through a smile.

"That drug dealing pretty boy." Samara giggled.

"No. When Donté told me what was going on, and I told him about himself, that was the last time we've spoken."

"He told me about that conversation. He said that he pretended that he was going home, but he waited in the cut to make sure that pretty boy didn't get out of line."

Samara had a huge smile on her face after hearing that information.

"That was my man. He wouldn't let no one even get rowdy with me, let alone hurt me." She sighed. "Donté."

"I know. I taught him well," he said before he redirected. "Look, Samara, when my brother told me what you were about and the things you've done for him, not to mention how well you carried yourself, I knew I was in love. When he told me how good you looked I thought that he was playing with me. Now that I see all of the above is true, I really need to get to know you."

"Are you sure you aren't just hitting on me because you were in prison and you haven't seen a woman in a while?" Samara joked with him. He smiled.

"I don't know if my brother told you or not, but before I got arrested I had been celibate for almost a year. These trollops I kept getting involved with weren't worth my time or energy. I wanted a real woman who wanted more out of life than materialism, sex, and drama. I wanted someone with a good heart who wanted to help our people. I never thought that person would be under forty and attractive, but here you are. Samara, we're going to move the world together. I need you in my life, and although I know you are an independent, very strong, black woman, you need me. So we need to go out and get to know each other, because I'll be around."

Samara smiled before her expression turned to confusion.

"Are you asking me out at your brother's funeral?" Mike laughed.

"No, I'm fulfilling his wishes. He liked you when y'all first met, but then he started to look at you like a big sister. The second time he told me about you, he was trying to sic me on you. He was like, 'Mike, she's the one. You stopped having sex just to look for the one. I've found her.' He really wanted us to be together. So now that I know he's looking down on us, I thought this was one of the best ways to make him happy."

"Your brother was right about something else. He told me that he couldn't wait for me to meet you. He told me I would love you. He was talking about where your head was at, but I can see it being both with time. I want to get to know you, too, Mike. I think we'll be all right."

He nodded and smiled.

"I know we will."

Chapter Twenty-Five

Whip Appeal

The day after the funeral Samara, Tonya, and Mike were at the center bright and early. There was plenty of work to be done that day. Besides preparing the morning breakfast and events for the day, they had to set up a memorial for Donté.

Mike was very impressed by what he saw in the center. Donté had already told him about the things they did daily, but seeing it firsthand was something different. It was as if he were dreaming.

The kids, who he remembered cursing in front of adults and vandalizing any and everything as a matter of habit, sat attentively, ready to learn and have fun. Their parents, who he remembered partying, smoking, and drinking, were in the center eating breakfast with their children. Some would be taking GED and basic computer literacy classes a little later in the day. Others were there for job training. Samara was forcing a community that everyone, including the residents, had written off, to believe.

After Samara and Mike finished erecting a small

memorial of pictures and quotes in honor of Donté just outside the basketball court, Samara walked toward the conference room to prepare it for the day's event. Tonya intercepted her.

"How are you doing, Ms. Brown? Is that you?" Tonya asked as she shot a glance over at Mike.

Samara smiled and nodded slowly.

"Yeah, that's me. I got that."

"Girl, he finer than Craig and he's cut up. How do you think you're going to keep snatching up the best for yourself and leave with the garbage?"

"I wasn't looking for these men. They came looking for me. Besides, he's the first ten I've come across. Craig is some garbage. You can have him. I think Mike may just be what I was looking for subconsciously. I'm trying to see what he's about."

"I can tell you for sure, unless he's a homo thug, he's going to need a heavy dose of the prescription," Tonya said, teasing her.

Samara playfully slapped her on the shoulder.

"Girl, you better stop. For your info, he was celibate before he went in."

Tonya looked over at Mike with shock showing on her face. "Naw. He could be a model or a male stripper. He's too fine. I know he has women chasing him. If you weren't blocking, I would have already put my bid in. Either he's lying or he's short."

Samara was confused. She glanced over at Mike who was easily taller than six feet. She turned back to Tonya, who nodded and winked. Samara's eyes bulged wide.

"Girl, you are terrible," Samara said, after catching on to Tonya's meaning. "Hey, you haven't seen his print through those jeans?"

Tonya nodded. "Yeah, I have. He must be lying then," Tonya said. They giggled and looked over at Mike. He turned and caught them staring at him. Mike smiled and they laughed even harder.

The day went well. The tribute for their fallen star caused a few tears, but mostly smiles and joy. They had T-shirts with photos of Donté posing in front of the center. Underneath his picture the words read, THE DONTÉ MCMILLAN COMMUNITY CENTER.

With the blessing of her mother, Marcus, Mike, and Donté's mother, Samara had decided to name the center after her apprentice, rather than her teacher. Everyone loved the idea, and there was already a work order to replace the sign above the center with Donté's name. There was nothing but celebration for Donté.

As Samara spoke to Stacy after the tribute, Craig entered the center. He caught Stacy's attention. She interrupted Samara mid sentence.

"I hope your old boyfriend realizes that you've moved on, or at least are trying to move on. If it gets ugly, I got my money on Mike."

Samara turned to see what Stacy was talking about. She saw Craig looking around for her. After he spotted her he began walking toward her. She looked over at Mike, who had taken notice of Craig. After seeing him head toward Samara, he put two and two together and headed to intercept Craig. Samara headed straight for Mike.

She stopped him, stared him in the eyes, and said very slowly, "Mike, I got this." He frowned and turned around, heading back to where he was before. Samara approached Craig and escorted him out the door.

"What do you want, Craig?" she asked once they were outside.

"You, Samara," he pleaded. "I need you in my life. I'm not really into this drug thing too tough, and I would gladly give it up for you."

"You don't need to do it for me. Some of these kids are barely surviving because their parents spend their money for food on the drugs you sell."

"I didn't really think about that. I thought about—"

"You," Samara interjected. "All you thought about was you."

"I know, but all I can think about now is you. If I have to get out of the game to get you back in my life, then I'm done."

I must have really put it on him, Samara thought. She believed that Craig had been thinking about her, but she doubted that he would really leave the game.

There was a moment of silence. Craig looked down at her shirt with the photo of Donté and shook his head.

"I really liked Tay. He was a good dude. I just wish . . . he had stayed out of those neighborhood beefs."

Samara picked up on his hesitation. The ending of his statement wasn't what he had in mind.

"So, are we friends? Can we have a friendly dinner?" Craig asked.

Samara was still trying to figure out Craig's angle, but she didn't want him to realize that. "I don't know. Are your business partners just going to let you leave that money on the table?"

"Yeah. That's something I'm going to have to work on. I think if I pull one more move for them and give them most of my cut, then they'll let me out. They'll probably expect some favors when I go to the NBA, though." Samara pursed her lips as if she thought that wasn't a likely scenario. "I'm going have to step my man up into my position. They'll be all right without me."

"They sure will," Samara agreed with a sinister smile. "They sure will."

Chapter Twenty-Six

The Cleaner

Samara had promised herself and her mother that she would try to use her head to overcome problems, rather than her piece, but she had to make another exception. Donté was dead, and now that she had figured out who killed him and why, there was work to be done. In fact, she could kill at least two birds with one stone on this mission. She could get rid of the coward who had ordered the hit on her apprentice, and also kill the local supplier.

Samara was so swift that Craig never realized that she had picked up on his hesitation when he was speaking about Donté's death. She had quickly filled in the pieces to what Craig hadn't said. After Donté told Samara that Craig was deep in the drug game, Samara had confronted Craig and told him that she didn't ever want to see or speak to him again. She had also warned him that if he continued to sell drugs he would be dealt with. Craig obviously figured out that Donté had put his business out there since Donté was the only person in Samara's life who knew about Craig's secret. Therefore, Craig was looking to put Donté out of business for ruining his chances with Samara. But Craig messed up by not realizing that Samara was all about business.

After speaking with Craig, Samara left Tonya in charge of the center so she could leave early that day. She had to track Craig and disrupt the transaction that she knew was set to take place. Maybe she could put a dent in the area's drug trade for a little while, maybe long enough to gain more ground in the community for the center and its programs. Either way, she couldn't see Craig making it out of the situation alive.

Samara had given J-Rock money to buy a cheap, used car from the neighborhood car dealer who had a dealer's license and purchased the cars from an auction in Pennsylvania. The early eighties Cadillac Seville came with illegally obtained paper tags and tinted windows. It was perfect for Samara's mission, although it was a magnet for police looking to make a traffic stop.

Samara pulled up to the end of Craig's block and saw his car posted out front. He stayed in an apartment on Fourteenth Street near Walter Reed, far removed the ghettoes where he slung his dope. Samara had been patiently waiting in the car for nearly an hour while the sun completely faded and the street lights were the only thing to illuminate the area. She noticed a Cadillac Escalade pull up and four tough looking men get out. One of the men carried a duffel bag.

Samara would have to improvise. She expected that she would have to follow Craig to a neutral destination. She had no idea that he was stupid enough to be conducting business at his residence. But the more Samara thought about it, that probably wasn't even his place. It was probably a place where he took his female acquaintances and made drug deals. Either way, it was a dangerous way to conduct business.

At least Samara knew that Craig was telling the truth when he told her that this would be his last deal. Samara was there to make sure of that.

Samara considered the situation. There were at least five men in the apartment, and no doubt that all of them were armed. She had plenty of bullets for them all, including any of Craig's associates who were already there. She drove around the block and parked in an alley.

Exiting the car dressed in all black and sporting fake dreadlocks, shades, a ball cap, a mustache, and a beard, Samara entered the code she had seen Craig use to open the door entry system without a key. She crept up the stairs, and after taking a quick glance down the hallway, she saw two guys outside of the apartment having a casual conversation. She had seen both of them get out of the Escalade.

Samara extracted her two .40-caliber Glock 22s and headed down the hall. She spoke in a deep, manly voice.

"Y'all know what it is. Get on the ground!"

The men were shocked to see what they thought was a man approaching them with two guns. One of them didn't take heed, but reached for his gun. *Boom! Boom! Boom! Boom!* Two shots from each gun left two men on the ground with two shots to the chest. She stood over them and delivered one shot to each of their heads.

She turned the handle to the apartment door, opened it, and quickly turned and ran back down the hallway. The people inside the apartment fired a combined thirty rounds as soon as the door opened. One of the men inside peeked outside and saw no one except two dead men on the floor.

"Fuck! Somebody got Sam and Dub. We got to get out of here," Treach said.

"You don't see nobody out there?" a voice from inside the apartment asked.

"Naw. They must've run off. We gotta get out of here right now. The cops will be here any minute now."

"Did somebody follow you up here?" Craig asked Treach from inside the apartment.

"Nigga, ain't nobody follow me. Is someone looking for you?" Treach tossed the suspicion right back at Craig. So there they stood, Craig and his man, along with Treach and his man. There was no trust and four guns among them.

"Man, fuck it. We gotta get out of here," Craig said to his man and grabbed the product. Treach and his man grabbed the money and the four ventured into the hallway, nervous as hell. They made their way for the stairwell. As soon as Treach stepped through the stairwell doorway, he caught two in the face. The three remaining men ran back down the hallway.

Samara entered the stairwell doorway. Treach's partner in crime, Z, realized that the money lay beside Treach. He couldn't see his man dying and a hundred thousand in cash go to waste like that. He slowly walked toward the stairwell. He stood ten feet from the door with his gun at the ready. Sirens began to blare in the distance.

Realizing that her time was limited, Samara grabbed the bag of money and hoisted it into the hallway. Z fired three shots at the duffel bag, thinking it was the assailant. Samara stuck her gun outside the door and blindly fired two shots. Z fired until his gun clicked.

Samara entered the hallway and shot the fleeing Z twice in the back. Craig was nowhere to be found, and the sirens continued to get louder.

Samara ran down the stairs and out the back door. She saw Craig and his man getting into a Jeep Cherokee. She fired at them, hitting Craig's man, who slumped over beside the SUV. Craig hopped in the driver's seat and turned the ignition. Samara ran up on him. Just as he shifted the Cherokee into gear, Samara placed her last two bullets into the windshield, tagging Craig once in his left shoulder and once in the chest. The car suddenly swerved toward Samara. She attempted to dive out of the way, but the small truck hit her and knocked her about five feet away. Both of her guns fell, and her hat and wig flew off. A few seconds later, the Cherokee came to a screeching halt. Samara was hurt, but managed to get up. Craig stomped on the accelerator and sped off.

Samara's leg was badly bruised by the fall, but she managed to hobble over to her old Cadillac and pull off. The police and EMS were inside the building. Craig was gone and Samara knew she wouldn't catch up with him that night. She was about three blocks away from the scene when the police finally secured the entire building and the block it encompassed. Samara escaped, but she was disgusted. The reason for the mission was to take out Craig, and even though she had shot him, he was the only person who had survived. A failed mission meant that there was another one forthcoming, according to her daddy's rules.

Chapter Twenty–Seven

Plight of the Digital Versatile Disc

A few days later, Samara prepared herself for the council hearing to determine the fate of the center. She had just spoken to Tonya, who was about to pick up Marcus, Stacy, and her mother from her mother's house. Samara was going to pick up Mike and J-Rock. She had just put on her clothes and was preparing to take care of her hair when the front door came crashing in.

Samara ran into her bedroom and dove across the bed, falling onto the other side. She reached underneath her bed and extracted her AR-15 assault rifle. She chambered a round and held her gun at the ready.

"Police! Police! We have a search warrant," a male voice yelled. Samara heard the pitter patter of boots walking around on the first floor and some ascending the stairs. She held her gun at the ready, ducking behind her bed. If it were the police, she needed visual verification. If it was not, shame on the first person who stepped through that door.

A tactical officer stuck his head in and out of the

bedroom door in a split second and saw Samara poised to do damage.

"Samara, drop the gun!" he yelled.

"Show me your badge," Samara yelled back.

"Drop the gun," another officer yelled. "This is your final warning."

"Your partner saw what I'm holding. You can come in here with that bullshit if you want to. I won't be the only one dying in here today. If y'all are really police officers, all I want to see is a badge. I'll toss my gun on the bed and place my hands in the air. I need to see a badge."

"OK. OK. I'm going to extend my badge into the doorway." The officer did as he said. The badge looked genuine from twelve feet away. He quickly pulled back the badge and reiterated his demand. "Drop the gun." Samara placed the gun on the bed and placed her hands in the air. The officer did another sneak peak and saw that Samara had cooperated. He entered with his gun drawn. Two more officers entered the bedroom with their guns drawn on her.

"Turn around and back up toward me," the officer ordered. Samara did as she was told. One of the officers grabbed the rifle. The other kept his gun trained on Samara's head. The one who was giving the commands placed her in handcuffs. Pressing his manhood against her soft and perfectly shaped butt, he felt for any other weapons. He checked her breasts and her crotch thoroughly for any weapons. She already felt violated by the way he was feeling on her, but when she felt his manhood becoming erect she knew he was getting out of hand.

"Is all that necessary?" she asked as she stepped away. "I don't have any other weapons." She saw lust in his eyes.

"I got to make sure. Not many people, especially women, keep weapons like this in their homes. You're dangerous," the officer said, smiling. "I got make sure you don't have any other guns or knives on you."

"Well if you're still not convinced, then you need to send a female officer in here to check me. If I get groped again, I'm filing an assault charge," Samara said very sternly. The officer's smile faded fast.

"Take her downstairs," the officer in charge said.

"I need to see a copy of that search warrant," Samara said as she was led downstairs. The officer ignored her and began to toss the place. When she got downstairs there were three more officers going through her things. She could hear other officers rumbling through her stuff in the basement. "I need to see a copy of that warrant," Samara repeated. The officer who led her down the steps made her sit on the couch. As if on cue, a police lieutenant entered the house and sat beside Samara.

"Good morning, Ms. Brown," the man said.

Samara looked at his rank and his nameplate.

"Good morning, Lieutenant Snow. Do you mind telling me what all this is about?"

"I'll tell you everything," the officer said. "Just give my officers a few moments to do their jobs, and then I'll tell you everything." Samara didn't want to wait for an explanation, but she knew there wasn't much of an alternative. The actual warrant would say what they were looking for, but the lieutenant why. Besides, she was lining up her curse words as the seconds went by. Samara's house phone rang, and everyone ignored it. The caller hung up without leaving a message.

The officers that were upstairs brought down Samara's computer and a bag of CDs and DVDs. The officer who had sexually harassed Samara came up to the lieutenant and said, "I think we got it. We found two of them unlabeled. One was hidden in a box inside the closet. The other was in her purse."

Samara was stunned by what she heard.

"What in the hell is going on here?" she asked. Her question was ignored.

"Hey everybody, we got what we need. Let's wrap it up," the officer yelled to the other officers who were sifting through her stuff throughout the house. One of the officers came upstairs from the basement with a shotgun.

"I got a shotgun from downstairs," the officer said.

"I found a Tec-9 in the kitchen," another officer said.

"Plus she's got an AR-15 upstairs and what looks like a government issued gas mask and bulletproof vest, lieutenant," the officer in charge upstairs said. "She threatened to let us have it if we didn't show her a badge."

"I legally own those rifles and the shotgun according to the laws of the District of Columbia. The mask and vest are none of your business," Samara responded.

"I don't remember seeing those during the first search," the lieutenant said to Samara. He turned his attention to his officers. "Just leave them be," he said. "I'll be out there in a few," he said to the officer in charge. The officers put down the guns and all of them left the house.

"Can you remove these cuffs?" Samara asked, and the lieutenant complied. "First off, why was it necessary to destroy my door?"

"We couldn't have you attempting to destroy evidence."

"Evidence of what?"

"Well there's evidence of money laundering and conspiracy to distribute narcotics."

"Lieutenant, that's bullshit, and you know it. And if that's the case, why wait until this morning to come get that evidence? Lieutenant, I'm not stupid. I know that y'all have not come looking for evidence of me being part of some criminal enterprise that you know does not exist. You know as well as I do that your officers planted those drugs at the center."

The officer sat back and smiled as Samara spoke.

"Those are pretty strong allegations you're making."

"It ain't a damn allegation," Samara said before pausing. "That officer was looking for CDs and DVDs. Taking my computer is just a cover up. Those two disks he was talking about showed your officers planting that evidence. This raid was just to make sure that I didn't bring those DVDs to the hearing today."

"Those are some even harsher allegations, but pretty perceptive. All of these charges are going to go away once the center is closed. I like you, Ms. Brown. You're a good woman with a good heart. You just got caught up in the middle of some petty people's bullshit. Just let the center go and try again in a few years."

"I'm not letting shit go. That's my center and no one's going to take it from me. You police officers are unbelievable. The center has helped decrease the flow of drugs and violence in the area and yet you're in with the politicians to try to shut it down."

"I got a job to do. When you've been in city government as long as I have, you learn that you have to have some friends. Those friends can help you out of a jam and vice versa. You're young now. We you get a little older you'll understand. You can't expect that you're going to do things your way and say fuck everyone else and that those people aren't going to try to force your hand. It's the way of the world. You just rubbed the wrong people a little too early in the game."

"Hey, lieutenant," Samara said.

"Yes, Ms. Brown?"

"Fuck 'em, and fuck you too. You're one of them. I

hope y'all didn't think that was my last hope. I'll see you at the hearing and then I'll see all of you bastards in court or in front of Congress. Now get the fuck out of my house." Samara was livid, evidenced by her fluid use of profanity.

"Hey, Ms. Brown, we've already got the copies your friend Tonya had at her place a few minutes ago," the lieutenant said as he watched her feistiness disintegrate into disappointment. "It doesn't have to be hard, Ms. Brown. They're going to close the center anyway. It's probably best if you don't even show up at the hearing. Just try again in a few years."

Samara was sad. She had nothing else to say to the officer. He got up and exited the house. She sat back down on the couch and placed her face in her hands. *Things looked so good for the center twenty minutes ago,* Samara thought. Now she considered whether it was even worth it to go to the hearing at all.

It took Samara about fifteen minutes to get herself together. She went to secure her weapons and called Tonya, but got no answer. She called Mike to tell him what had happened. He was very upset. She told Mike she would pick him up in thirty minutes. He told her that he and J-Rock would at her place in fifteen.

When they arrived they helped put the door that was knocked from its hinges back into place. They put some furniture behind it to keep anyone from entering her home while they were at the hearing. Just as they prepared to leave Samara called her mother's house.

"Hello," Natalie answered.

"Hey, Ma, have you heard from Tonya?"

"Yes. I spoke to her a little while ago. She told me that the police raided her house. She said they probably raided yours, too, but she called you and you didn't answer, so she assumed that you left before they got there. I'm going to bring Marcus and Stacy. She said she'll meet us there."

"OK, Ma. I'll see you there," Samara said and hung up.

About twenty minutes later Samara, Mike, and J-Rock caught up with Marcus, Stacy, and Natalie. Samara explained how the police had used the searches to weaken her case against the closing. At that point, all Samara had was allegations. Tonya was not at the hearing yet, and that worried Samara. They entered the council chambers and began the process of closing the Donté McMillan Community Center.

The DC government, including the police department and social services voiced their many concerns with the center. They pointed out the shootings outside and inside the center, along with the stabbing of its founder. They asserted that the center was no safer than a nightclub, thus making it unfit for children or young adults. They also argued that the discovery of drugs on the premises indicated that the center might be a front for criminal activity because it did not use any government funding to support it. The center's opponents went on for about forty-five minutes telling why the center needed to be closed. It wasn't looking good for the center.

Then the councilman for Ward 4, who sponsored the meeting, ordered Samara to come up and testify. People were set to testify on behalf of Samara and the center, but the councilman had other plans. He needed Samara to step up, get embarrassed, and get out of the building. The government had presented an excellent case, and Samara had no proof to the contrary. He was trying to put an end to her misery as fast as possible.

"Good morning, Ms. Brown," the councilman said.

"Good morning, council, and all attendees here," Samara responded.

"Ms. Brown, the government has presented a very strong case as to why this center should be closed, and why you and some of your cohorts may be facing criminal charges. What do you have to say about these allegations?"

"First and foremost, all allegations that count us as criminals are blatant lies. Moreover—" Samara said before being interrupted by the councilman.

"Do you have any proof to back that up?" he asked.

"I've got proof. It's on the discs that the police came and confiscated this morning to make sure they didn't make it to this meeting. They showed the police planting drugs in the center and carrying them out like they had just found the drugs there. This whole thing is a setup, run by you and Ms. Simms over there," she said, pointing to the councilman and then to the white woman representing Change for Urban America. "They want to force me out of the center and make it their own center." There was a collective sigh in the audience.

"What proof do you have for these outlandish allegations?"

"The proof you sent Lieutenant Snow and his boys to confiscate."

"So you have no proof. Did we also orchestrate the violence that occurs inside and outside the center? Can you show me how the center is in any way, shape, or form suitable for children to be there?" the councilman challenged her.

"We've had some setbacks as far as violence is concerned, but since the center opened four months ago, all crime, including shooting, stabbings, robberies, and drug possession has been reduced by more than sixty percent as compared to any six-month period since you've been in office. That's according to your police department's stats. I don't know what you've been doing for the last seven years, but crime hasn't fallen in that neighborhood until the center opened," Samara said with every bit of sarcasm she could muster. There was a roar among the crowd.

The council chairwoman ordered everyone to settle down, and the councilman continued.

"Madam Chairwoman, Ms. Brown has all of these words but no proof. She has no video, and she did not bring these crime statistics with her to back up her assertions. The government has laid out an overwhelming case against Ms. Brown and the center. I motion that we put its closure to a vote."

"Ms. Brown, with all of the other matters we have before us today, unless you can give us evidence to the contrary, or some corroborated testimony from an unbiased source, I'm going to put the motion to a vote," the council chairwoman said.

Samara's heart dropped. She knew the truth just as the councilman who was putting her out of business did, but she was a moment or two away from the permanent closure of the center. Samara was speechless.

"Ms. Brown?" the council chairwoman asked.

"Can we postpone the vote for one week so I can get my evidence together?" Samara sounded like a child who had forgotten her homework.

"She's had more than two weeks already. We have other business to attend to. I say we vote," the councilman suggested. Just at that moment the door to council chambers opened. The councilman's eyes bulged with surprise when he saw Tonya.

"I'm sorry, Ms. Brown. I'm putting the matter of the closure of the Future Leader's Community Center—"

Samara, Mike, Marcus, Stacy, and J-Rock stood as Tonya walked toward Samara. They all said together, correcting the councilwoman, "The Donté McMillan Community Center." Following their example, a fourth of the audience stood and chanted the same phrase.

"Settle down, everyone. Settle down or we'll start removing people," the chairwoman said. Samara turned around and motioned for the members of the audience on their feet to settle down. Tonya handed Samara a disc and both sat down.

"All in favor of the closure," the chairwoman said as ten of the thirteen council members raised their right hands and said aye. The councilman smiled, humming as he voted for the closure.

"Madam Chairwoman, I have the video," Samara blurted out during the voting.

"She can't interrupt the vote," the councilman protested.

"Ms. Brown, if you interrupt again, you will be removed and arrested for disorderly conduct," the chairwoman warned.

"It's OK. I'll let the media have this disc that shows the police department committing felonies and let the council explain to Congress why they sided with the criminal acts of the police instead of looking at the evidence for themselves."

The entire room was silent until the councilman shouted, "She can't come in here threatening us. She's the criminal. Have that woman arrested for interrupting the vote again." Lieutenant Snow ordered an officer to remove Samara from the room. Again there was again silence in the room save for a low murmur among the audience.

Just as the officer was about to place Samara in handcuffs, the chairwoman said, "Hold on, officer. Ms.

Brown, if what you say is not on that disc, you're going to jail for a lot more than disorderly conduct." Lieutenant Snow looked nervous.

"I object to this break in council procedures. According to procedures—" the councilman began.

"Be quiet, councilman. I've heard enough from you. I know the rules. I also know that as chairwoman I can run this hearing as I see fit. If there is nothing on the disc, she's going to jail. If there is proof of what she says, then we need to do an investigation into the conspiracy. Either way, we're watching the disc. Ms. Brown, you have five minutes to show us your proof."

Tonya popped the DVD into a nearby player and readied it to the exact point where the officers unloaded the drugs in the center and then pretended to find them. Everyone in the room was stunned. Samara and Tonya were loving it. The councilman looked like he was going to pull out his hair.

"After these revelations, we're going to postpone the vote for thirty days as we look into the criminal activity detailed on this disc," the chairwoman said to the delight of the crowd.

After everyone left the room, Samara was approached by Officer Presto, the female officer with whom Samara had a few bad encounters in the past.

"I know we've had our differences, but I had no idea about the setup. I asked the lieutenant about the allegations and he said"—the officer paused and Samara looked at her curiously—"'I'll get back with you about that.' I like what you've done for the community, but you're just so sassy."

"Look who's talking," Samara said with a smile.

"If you ever need my help with your center, I'm here. I'll try not to be ignorant again," the officer stated, and this time they both smiled.

Chapter Twenty-Eight

Check Out Time

The next couple of days went well for Samara and the center. The hearing garnered top news coverage, including front page on *The Washington Post* and *The Washington Times*. The police department was under heavy scrutiny, and the councilman whom Samara had implicated was put under investigation by the Metropolitan Police Department. The feds even said they would look into the case. Samara and the center had been all but exonerated from the allegations they faced before the hearing. Even better, donations to the center increased sevenfold.

Samara still had an unresolved issue—Craig. He had survived the attack and was in the hospital under police watch. Samara had recuperated well from being hit by the truck, and unfortunately Craig was healing too. He was in stable condition according to the men's basketball coach with whom Samara had spoken. Samara attempted to see him, but she was not on his visitor's list. She wanted to determine whether he would make it and if he had recognized her as his attacker. His long pause in the alley after half of her disguise flew off made her apprehensive.

A few days after the hearing Samara and Mike had their first official date. They had dinner at the Friday's on Pennsylvania Avenue near George Washington University. Soon after they were seated, Mike began the interrogation.

"Samara, how did you become the woman you are?" he asked.

"Over a period of time," she said. He just stared at her, waiting for her to continue. "What do you mean?"

"I mean, you're so much different than any woman I've ever met. You care about the kids and the community more than yourself. You're one of the smartest women I've come across, and you handle yourself better than some of the people I was locked up with. Donté never said that you carried guns because our conversations were monitored, but he implied it. He also said that you could box and knew martial arts. How does a twenty-one-year-old woman, fresh out of college act like a cross between a psychology professor, a Black Panther, and a Navy SEAL?"

Samara spoke in a very hushed tone.

"My daddy was a Ranger. He taught me everything the Army taught him. My mother has a couple of degrees, including ones in psychology and business administration. She has a master's in accounting. She originally planned on being a social worker to help our people, but when she did an internship and saw the BS and bureaucracy, and realized how the system was in place to keep the people in check, she changed her mind. She saw that the primary troubles our people faced were with finances or economic oppression, so she went into accounting to learn the tricks of the people with the money."

"So you're the product of your parents, huh? One taught you force, and the other taught you a game plan and to care for your people," Mike said.

"My daddy cared for the people, too. He just went about it in a different way. I'll explain it to you one day."

"You've already accomplished so much at such a young age. What more do you have in mind? A second center?"

"A thousand centers. We're going to take this model across the country. We're going to put a stranglehold on the system that keeps up down and out. We're going to become a force like we once were, before some of us got ahead and thought we were better than the rest. We need unity to overcome, and I'll die trying to make that happen," Samara said with a seriousness that made her statement undeniable.

"I hear you, baby girl. I'm right with you. I would have done anything to see Donté become the man you helped him to become. We'll make a generation of leaders who want more, and let them go out and teach others to do the same. I know that those types of movements have failed before, but they didn't have the resources and rights that we have now. And more importantly, they didn't have Mike and Samara McMillan," Mike said with a huge grin. Samara was dumbfounded by Mike's bold statement.

"Mike, what in the hell are you talking about?" she asked, but Mike just smiled.

Later that evening Samara slept peacefully in her bed, dreaming about her and Mike being together. She was falling for Mike fast and hard. After just one date and one hug, she thought she was in love. Suddenly her dream was disrupted by the sound of breaking glass.

Samara jumped out of the bed, reached under the bed, and retrieved the AR-15. She ran to the window and caught a man in the act of tossing another Molotov cocktail into her home. The smoke had already begun to rise upstairs. Samara chambered a round and lifted the window and screen. By the time she got her gun outside the window the car was speeding away. She let about seven rounds go before the car was out of range. She was sure that she had hit the car at least a few times.

The smoke inside the house got very thick, very fast. Samara had to get out of the house quickly. She slid on her shoes and retrieved her gas mask from the closet just as the smoke began to invade her room. She placed on some loose fitting pajama pants and left the room. The heat and smoke were nearly unbearable. She ran down the stairs with her purse on her arm, a gas mask on her face, and a rifle in her hands. As she made her way downstairs she found her living room partially engulfed in flames. She had to hop over the banister a few steps short of the floor because of the heat emanating from the living room and the front door. She quickly ran to the back door and outside the house.

Once outside, she removed the gas mask and looked for a target. Anything that moved was subject to get it. She watched dejectedly as the house she had rented since her freshman year at Howard was consumed by fire. Tears welled up as memories began to float through the air in the form of ashes. Samara moved away from the house and into the alley, lugging her rifle with her. In the distance she could the roar of fire engines rushing to the scene. She went farther down the alley and hid the gun.

Watching her house go up in flames, she had forgotten all about her neighbors in the adjoining row houses. She ran out of the alley around to the front of the house to make sure everyone had made it out of their houses. The fire engines had just pulled up and were hooking their hoses up to the fire hydrants. Samara saw the families from the houses on both sides of her waiting in the street in their nightclothes. They looked very worried until they saw Samara. Everyone became happy and started crying because they were so glad to see that she was safe.

The firefighters began to douse the blaze when out of nowhere gunshots erupted. Everyone, including the firefighters, took cover and began looking around to see where the gunfire was coming from. There was a pause in the shooting.

"I had a couple of boxes of bullets upstairs in the front bedroom," Samara yelled to them, explaining the gunshots they heard.

After hearing Samara's explanation for the gunfire, the firefighters continued to battle the blaze. Fifteen minutes later they had the fire under control. The police had arrived, and they immediately began questioning Samara.

"What happened here?" a detective named Trent asked.

"Someone tried to kill me. They threw Molotov cocktails into my house."

"What's your name?" the detective asked and didn't immediately receive an answer. "Ma'am, what is your name?"

"Samara Brown."

The detective looked at her curiously. "So you're the one who brought all of that heat down on the department?"

"Well if those crooked bastards wouldn't have tried to set me up, there wouldn't be any heat on the department."

"Uh-huh. There were reports of gunshots. What do you know about that?" Samara hunched her shoulders.

"The only gunshots I heard were when the bullets exploded in my bedroom."

"The report of gunshots came about the same time as the call for the fire, not five or ten minutes ago."

"I don't know. Maybe the people who set my house on fire sent some rounds into my house as well. Did you ever think of that?"

"I'll tell you what I think. I think that you're guilty of unlawfully discharging a weapon. I think you're going to jail."

"I think you're as stupid as the cops who dropped the dope in the center. When you have evidence of the stuff you're talking about, then come see me. Otherwise, I'm done answering questions tonight. People came to my house and tried to murder me, and you didn't come here to find out about the perpetrators. You came here to harass me and get on my nerves. I don't have time," Samara said as she walked down the street and got into her car.

Fire engines and police cars lined the street, preventing her from leaving. She sat silently in her car, becoming distraught thinking about the tough times she had experienced during the last couple of weeks.

She had no idea who had burned down her house, but the list of possible suspects was short. It could have been some disgruntled police officers, or it might have been the councilman, who was not only about to lose his seat, but maybe his freedom as well. Outside of those people, the only other person who could have thought to do her harm was Craig. That was on the off chance that he actually realized she was the one who had shot him and killed his associates. Maybe he didn't forget the threat she made to ruin his business when she held him at gunpoint. Maybe when he put all the pieces together, he figured out that her agreeing to see him again was a setup move to make good on her threat. But whether Craig knew she was responsible was irrelevant. The outcome for him in her eyes would be the same. He was riding on borrowed time. If he didn't go to jail, he was going under some dirt.

About an hour later at two in the morning enough emergency service vehicles had moved for Samara to leave. She considered going to get her rifle, but thought better of it. She hadn't carried a pistol on her since she was stabbed and labeled a member of a criminal enterprise after they found drugs at the center. With the accusations ongoing, she received too much attention to carry a gun as she did in the past. Since handguns were illegal to possess in the city, she stored them and her other rifles and explosives in a secure vault she shared with her father at one of Rufus's friends' houses in Bowie, Maryland.

Samara drove away from her block, not really knowing where to go. She really wanted to be with Mike, but she didn't want to expose him to all of her troubles. Instead, she decided she would go to Tonya's house and stay the night. She hadn't even gotten three blocks away before a car with dark tinted windows pulled up behind her. Samara was very nervous. She didn't have any weapons or any way of protecting herself.

As Samara traveled along Florida Avenue, the car stayed about two car lengths behind her. She changed lanes from the left to the right, and the car stayed the same distance and did not change lanes. Samara made a sharp turn on Seventh Street. She looked in her rearview mirror, and a few seconds later she saw that the same car that was following her was now right behind her on Seventh Street. Once Samara was sure that she was being followed, she floored it. The other car also accelerated, trying to catch up with her. She ran all the lights, as did the car that was following her. If it were the police, they would have put the red flasher on the dash and pulled her over by then, because she had committed numerous traffic violations. She figured the person or people pursuing her were not the police, and to her their intentions seemed to include violence as the ending to the entire scenario.

Samara pushed her little Cadillac hard, traveling upward of sixty miles an hour on Georgia Avenue, flying past the center. The other car was still in hot pursuit. The cars picked up the attention of a squad car traveling in the opposite direction, and the officer immediately turned on the flashing lights and sirens upon seeing the chase. Samara turned right on New Hampshire Avenue, still traveling very fast with the other car still in pursuit, and the squad car following behind both speeding vehicles.

Suddenly Samara slammed on the brakes and made a sharp right onto Randolph Street. The driver of the car that was chasing Samara must have realized that if he tried to slow down to make the turn, he might never lose the police car, so the car kept straight with the police hot on its trail.

Finally Samara slowed down and hit a few side streets before making her way over to Tonya's house where she stayed the night.

Chapter Twenty-Nine

The Better Hand

Samara and Tonya awoke early the next morning. Samara was preparing herself so that she could open the center. Tonya told her that she and Stacy could handle it, and that Samara needed the day to get her life in order. Samara would have none of it. She was going to open the center that day as she had any other day. She refused to let outside influences dictate when and how she ran the center. Tonya informed her that she wasn't in it alone.

Samara had spoken to her mother, brother, Stacy, and Mike in the wee hours of the morning after she had arrived safely at Tonya's place. Each one of them insisted that they were on their way to see her, but she declined. Samara told them she would see them at the center in the morning, although each of them advised her against it.

Samara and Tonya didn't talk about the incident when she arrived, because Samara had already had a tough time, and Tonya figured when she was ready to talk to her, she would. Samara was taking too long for

Tonya's liking, so she proceeded to question Samara as they were getting dressed.

"Maury, who do you think it was?"

Samara paused before responding. "You don't want to know."

"Actually, I do. Who?"

"I think it was some of Craig's associates."

Tonya was amazed. "Are you serious? Why do you think he had something to do with it? Did you put it on him that bad that he would rather see you dead than not with him?"

Samara burst into laughter. It took her half a minute to stop laughing enough to answer her.

"Girl, you're crazy. I told you what happened that night when I told him I didn't want to see him anymore, right?"

"Somewhat. You said you held him at gunpoint with his own gun and told him you didn't want to see him again."

Samara nodded. "I also told him that if he didn't retire voluntarily, he would be forced out. He threatened me and my life, too, and that was that."

Tonya's eyes bulged and mouth dropped.

"Maury, you're the one who tried to murder Craig a few days ago?"

"I did. That bastard was the only one who survived. He hit me with his truck and made part of my disguise come off. Between that and my threat, he must have figured it was me, or that I put someone up to it."

"Why in the hell did you do that?" Tonya asked, still amazed. "You should've listened to your mother at the hospital. Violence doesn't solve all problems. You need to slow down, Samara. You can't just go around killing off your problems and think that there won't be any consequences. What's happened to you?"

Samara looked like a child who had been rebuked. Tonya was starting to sound like her mother.

"Look, Tonya, I think he had Donté killed. I wasn't willing to let that go."

"Why do you think that?"

"Donté used to sell drugs, and Craig was his supplier. That day Craig came by and asked for another date and I agreed, until Donté told me what Craig was all about. That night I threatened Craig with his own gun, told him I didn't want to see him again, and told him to quit or else. A few days later Donté was murdered. I couldn't let it go."

"Samara, I loved Donté, too, and I want to see his killer brought to justice, but you can't keep playing judge, jury, and executioner. If you get caught or killed, what happens to the children who idolize you? How long do you think they're going to let me keep the center open? I thought we were doing all this to stop young, black males from murdering each other. We've gotten them to slow down in the area, and you've helped pick up the pace. Samara, don't you see? You're helping the system. You're murdering black males and have given up on rehabilitating or helping them. That's what the system does, and you're helping it to win."

Samara was devastated by Tonya's words. She left the room and sat on the stairs, considering her words. Tonya followed her.

"Samara, I understand your daddy taught you to be a mercenary, but why don't you hold those skills until they come for us? You do know that they're going to come for us, right?"

"Who's going to come for us, Tonya?"

"The system. They've already come for us a few times, but with limited violence. The more good we do, the more the system is going to attempt to push us into submission. Samara, we're trying to spark a revolution here. This country and the system make a habit of putting down revolutions with force, so you ought to save the GI Jane stuff for then. Let's cultivate minds for now. We'll teach them the tricks of the system that your mother has been teaching us since we were kids. We'll teach them to defend themselves along the way. But if you don't calm down, this revolution will end before it gets started good."

Samara smiled, got up from the stairs, and gave Tonya a hug.

"I love you, sis. I'm sorry that I've been so big headed and making moves without consulting you first. We're in this thing together. I'll come to you first before I decide to do something stupid so that you can talk me down. I can't believe that anger and arrogance blinded me to what I was doing. Here I think I'm doing good by my people to eliminate these problems, when I was actually doing the system a favor by keeping the cycle of killing going."

Tonya nodded. "It's OK, Maury. That's what friends are for. We're going to put a stranglehold on this system, but we have to do it together."

"Agreed."

Samara and Tonya arrived at the center just before eight in the morning, an hour before it was set to open. They were greeted by a host of media and police. Samara attempted to bypass them all when Lieutenant Snow stood in front of her, blocking her path.

The lieutenant smiled as he said, "Samara Brown, you're under arrest for unlawfully discharging a firearm, with more charges to follow." He nodded to an officer who placed her in handcuffs.

"This is bullshit," Tonya yelled.

"Don't worry about it, Tonya. I'll be back in a few hours. Just take care of the center." The media began shooting questions at Samara as the officer led her away from the center.

Lieutenant Snow turned to Tonya.

"We'll be back for you," he said.

"Fuck you," she responded violently. He laughed at her and walked away.

The officer led her to the lieutenant's unmarked police car and prepared to put her in the backseat. The lieutenant came over just in time to correct him.

"Naw, place her in the front," he said.

"What about the cuffs?" the officer asked.

"Put them in front of her," the lieutenant said before turning to her. "You are going to behave, right?" Samara ignored him. The officer removed the cuffs and placed them on with her arms in front of her. The lieutenant got in his car and they drove off.

"What are you doing, lieutenant?" Samara asked.

"Taking you to jail."

"Do you think those charges are going to fly?"

"Doesn't really matter. We've got some better charges than that. That's just for starters. You really caught us by surprise with that video. It's going to stink for a little while and maybe an officer will lose his job behind it, but we're gonna just make it harder on you," the lieutenant said.

"Why is it so important to hang me, lieutenant?"

"Samara, I like you. I wish you were a police officer, to be truthful, but then you wouldn't be you. Someone wanted the center closed. All you had to do was let the damn place close. But not only did you prevent it from closing, you made me and the department look bad in so doing. So it's no longer the councilman and his people against you. It's me and the department against you, and although you're up one, we have a much better hand than you. Since you want to play the game, we'll play the game."

"It's cool, lieutenant. I'm in it for the long haul. You are going to have to drag me away from the center kicking and screaming. I haven't come this far to be deterred. Those other charges better be pretty good," Samara said with indignation.

The lieutenant shook his head. "You're stubborn as hell, you know that." Samara nodded. "The other charges will put you down for anywhere from ten years to life. It's not looking good for you. I hate to do you like this, and although I wouldn't mind you getting that spineless-ass councilman, I can't see you defeating me."

"It's not about me and you. It's about good and evil. I'm trying to help people and you're trying to stop people from being helped. We'll let the Lord decide who's right and wrong."

"The Lord? I didn't realize you knew who that was. I thought it was in your guns you trusted," he said, shooting a glance over to Samara. She looked away. "Well, Ms. Brown, may the better person win, because I intend to see this through."

Samara looked him the eyes.

"I do too, lieutenant. In fact, I think y'all are overplaying your hand. As a matter of fact, I think y'all are simply outmatched. I'm going to have to suggest that y'all fold 'em while you still have the chance. "

The lieutenant was shocked. He pulled the car over to the side of the road and stared at her.

"You talk a really good game, young lady. If you can get the better of me in this game that I've been playing since you were a kid, then not only will I admit defeat, I'll get in your corner. But with the stakes so high, if I win, there will be no mercy."

"I don't need any mercy. All I need is for you to play fairly. I'll take care of everything else," Samara said with a huge grin on her face. The lieutenant laughed.

"I hope you aren't selling wolf tickets over there, because I'm about to put you in check."

"I'm a queen, stupid. You can only put a slow, lethargic king in check. Queens roam and wreak havoc. I'll learn you," Samara said to the lieutenant's delight. He was thoroughly entertained all the way to central processing.

About four hours later Tonya went down to the Superior Court building where Samara was arraigned and released on her own recognizance. They arrived at the center about fifteen minutes later. There was a lone police car in front of the building.

"Tonya, we have to keep our heads up. That lieutenant is going to be coming at us hard and fast. I egged him on and basically told him that he couldn't outsmart us, so he's going to try to make life hard for us for a little while. The future of the center and the youth all across this nation depend on us overcoming this battle. I know we can do it," Samara said to her best friend. Tonya smiled.

"I know we can, too. They're messing with two psychology alumnae from Howard. They don't know what they're getting themselves into." They both laughed. "All the same, girl, I guess you better bring me up to speed on self-defense, especially when it comes to firearms." Samara was pleasantly surprised.

"I got you. Just don't go out and become a vigilante or anything like that."

"Look who's talking," Tonya said. They got out of the car and headed for the center.

Officer Presto, the female who Samara had a few run-ins with since the center's opening, approached them. Tonya turned to Samara.

"Here comes that damn lady officer with the smart mouth," Tonya said.

"She acted like she was upset over the setup. She says she's on our side now. She might be playing the fifty. We'll have to feel her out," Samara said as Tonya nodded.

"Hey, Samara. Hi, Tonya. Can I talk to y'all inside the building?" Officer Presto asked. The trio entered the center, headed straight for Samara's office, and sat down.

"What's your first name, Officer Presto?" Samara asked.

"Deidre," the officer responded.

"What's on your mind, Deidre?" Samara asked.

"What I'm going to tell you, you didn't hear from me. In fact, after I tell you, you never heard it at all. I'm just giving you the heads up before they come, because what they are coming with is tough," the officer said. Both of the young women waited for Officer Presto to proceed. After a brief pause, she began to break it down for them.

"A few months ago Toni Blair got caught with an eighth a kilo of crack by some vice officers on a routine traffic stop. Toni Blair was Craig Miller's right-hand man. Toni started snitching immediately and sold Craig out. Instead of arresting Craig, the officers just sat back and watched his moves. They've been tracking him for a while now. They already had enough on Craig to sit him down for at least twenty years, but they wanted to catch him and his connection from New York in a transaction.

"All of that is important to you because while they were watching him, they saw you in the picture a few times," Deidre said, pointing at Samara. "Since then, you've become their enemy number one. Before the video surfaced, they were going to tie you to Craig and say that y'all were dealing dope together out of the center. But once the video surfaced, that took away that option. After the video erased the conspiracy, they had to find another way to get you.

"A few days ago, as you know, Toni Blair, the New York connection, and his man were murdered uptown in a drug deal gone bad. Craig was shot, but he survived. The death of their star informant, and the fact that Toni wasn't able to inform them about the transaction in time for them to set up surveillance devastated the case they were trying to build. But they still had enough on Craig to put him away for a while, so they offered him a deal while he was at the hospital. Implicate you"—Deidre pointed to Samara—"in his drug organization, and they'd make the charges against Craig just misdemeanors."

"Are you serious?" Tonya asked.

"The police are unbelievable," Samara said.

"Oh, that ain't nothing," Deidre said as she walked over and felt roughly on Samara's upper legs. Samara winced and pushed her hands away.

"What the hell is wrong with you?" Samara asked, standing.

Deidre just looked at her for a moment and then shook her head.

"While Craig was still under police supervision at the hospital, this idiot gets on the phone with one of his boys and starts talking about the shooting. He tells his man on a tapped phone that he hit the shooter with his truck and part of the disguise came off. He hated to admit it, but he thought the shooter was a female, and he thought he knew who she was," Deidre said evenly. "He wasn't stupid enough to say any names, but whether that person was you or not, and I'm sure it was you, the police are going to make you the shooter. They're trying to send you up for a triple homicide. You better get together an airtight alibi like right now, or it's not looking good for you."

Samara and Tonya both looked very concerned. The police had Samara in a very compromising position. The lieutenant wasn't bluffing. Samara had to try to think her way out of this situation, and fast.

"How do you know all this?" Samara asked.

"Lieutenant Snow and I participate in extracurricular activities every now and then," Officer Presto said with a slight smile. "He does a lot of talking afterward."

"There's no ring on your finger," Samara said as Deidre shook her head. "But I saw a wedding band on the lieutenant's finger."

"He's married. I'm his unofficial girlfriend. We fuck and he talks. He really admires you too, Samara. He said he wished y'all were on the same team, but since you've already made him look bad and challenged him, he's gotta make you look bad and win."

"Why are you telling us all of this?" Tonya asked.

"I'm telling you all this because I like Samara, too. I know we bumped heads a couple of times when we first met, but that's because we're both headstrong and stubborn. I know your heart is in the right place. You're just a little abrasive at times. I'm helping you because I like what the center has accomplished and I don't like the fact that they tried to close you down for

a shady councilman and some white people. The lieutenant didn't really want to do it, but the councilman
called in a debt owed to him. One hand washes the
other, ya know."

"I really appreciate all of the information and all of
the help, Deidre," Samara said as Tonya nodded in
agreement.

"Don't get me wrong, I don't endorse murder, but I
am also not going to pass judgment," Deidre said. "I
don't have evidence that you murdered anyone, but
there are some strong circumstances. Maybe you went
to play Robin Hood and the situation got out of hand. I
don't know, and I don't care. They justify it whenever a
police officer kills someone while on duty, so it is what
it is. But I will advise that if you ever use a gun again,
it better be in self-defense.

"The reason I'm helping you is because I see in these
kids and in this community what I've never seen before. I see hope in their eyes. And for that, you definitely deserve a second chance. Don't fail these kids,
like their parents, the government, and even the police
department has, Samara. Don't fail these kids."

Later that evening as Samara, Tonya, Stacy, Mike,
Marcus, and J-Rock closed the center, a car with
tinted windows pulled up. As each of them were walking to their cars, gunshots began to ring out from automatic weapons. After the car sped off, Tonya and Stacy
were stretched out on the ground suffering from multiple gunshot wounds. Samara was only grazed across
the shoulder, and Mike was hit in the leg. It was the beginning of Samara's breakdown.

Chapter Thirty

Have Faith

Samara stayed at the hospital all night long. Her wound was basically a scratch and burn across her shoulder. She refused treatment. She was there for her friends, who were in much worse shape than she was. Her brother and J-Rock were the only ones completely unscathed.

Samara's best friend Tonya was in bad shape. She caught three bullets—two in her abdomen and one in her leg. After hours of surgery, they managed to upgrade her status from grave to critical, but the doctors only gave her a fifty percent chance of making it, and a twenty percent chance of living a normal life again. Besides her injuries, Tonya had lost a lot of blood, which was a major concern for those charged with caring for her.

Stacy suffered shots to her chest, arm, and leg. She was also listed in critical condition, but by early the next morning she was upgraded to serious. Marcus was very distraught over the severe injuries to his girlfriend and to his sister, Tonya.

Mike took a bullet in the leg, but was in stable condition. His injury was not serious, just painful and inconvenient. He refused to stay in a hospital bed. Most of that night and early in the morning he was in a wheelchair sitting beside either Tonya or Stacy.

Samara was in her mother's arms off and on for hours. It was the first time in years that she needed to be cared for. For a very long time Samara had been totally independent and self-sufficient. No matter how bad the problem was, she would find a way to solve it on her own. But ever since J-Rock got shot, troubles had been coming consistently and had gotten progressively worse. Now with two of her closest friends and future boyfriend laid up in the hospital, she was unable to cope with all the troubles that had arisen. She was very upset over the fact that her actions had led to the death of Donté, and was the reason her friends were fighting for their lives. Even worse, she didn't know how to make it right. She was depressed and her super tough and sassy façade had washed away with the tears that lined her cheeks.

Natalie, who was also very distraught, had never seen her daughter so vulnerable—ever. When times were tough her daughter overcame. Natalie was really concerned about her daughter's mental state. It was good that Samara started showing some emotion in her life besides sass and anger, but she was in a shell now. Natalie wanted to make sure Samara didn't break and go on a murdering spree.

"Maury," Natalie called to her daughter.

Samara lifted her head from her mother's chest. Her eyes were blank and despondent. Her mother called her again, causing her snap out of the trance she seemed to be in and focus on Natalie.

"Yes, Ma."

"They're going to be fine, Samara. It's in God's hands now. We need to pray for them and let God do what he does. I have faith that they'll be fine," Natalie said. Samara nodded in agreement before laying her head on her mother's shoulder.

"Maury," her mother called to her again. Samara lifted herself up and looked her mother in the eye. "I know this is going to seem like a stupid question, but are you OK? I know these are people you really love who got hurt, and I love them too, like they were my own daughters, but you always shrugged off hard times and disappointment, no matter how bad it was. I'm just asking because I don't want you to hurt any-body or get yourself hurt. I've seen your father look the way you look only once. I was hoping to never see that look again."

Samara shrugged. "Ma, I love Tonya. She's my sister and now they're telling me she might not make it. I've already lost my daddy. My brother got hurt really bad a few months ago. Donté is dead. Stacy, who saved my life and who I was hoping would become my sister-in-law, is in bad shape. My boyfriend—" Samara started to say, then realized her slip. Natalie had a curious grin on her face. Samara finally smiled for the first time since the shooting took place. "My friend Mike is in here banged up. Things have just been so tough lately."

Natalie smiled. "The Lord never puts on you more than you can handle. Your daddy and I raised you strong to prepare you for the purpose God had for you. It looks like you've been ordained to change the world, and that's not an easy task. Challenges, no matter how tough, make us stronger, and since you've been charged with carrying the fate of the world on your back, that back needs to be pretty strong," Natalie said as Samara smiled.

The doctor came and told everyone waiting for the condition of Tonya that she had slipped into a coma and her prognosis had been downgraded to extremely critical. Samara began to weep. Natalie attempted to slow the tears that began to seep from her own eyes as she tried to console her daughter.

"It's just Satan trying to shake our faith, Maury. If we believe and pray, she'll be fine," Natalie said to her daughter, who didn't look so sure.

A few hours later Samara checked in to a hotel in Greenbelt, Maryland, wearing a disguise and using an alias. She entered with a few clothes she took from Tonya's house and her assault rifle in the oversized luggage case. Her mother wanted her to stay with her, but Samara refused. She needed time to herself. She needed time to decide if the life she lived was worth it.

Later that evening, as she listened to the storm outside, she considered committing suicide until the phone rang and she received a visit. Now she was looking forward to meeting her father, who she hadn't seen for more than a year.

As Samara sat in the hotel room, she considered how the ambience of the storm was in direct correlation with her life. Blacks, represented by the darkness, controlled the center. Whites, represented by the lightning, had tried to invade and take control of the room, which was the center. The thunder represented the threats, allegations, and violence that constantly rattled and shook the center and its members. Much like that night, Samara was destined to weather the storm. Thoughts of suicide were now banished from her mind. All she could think about was seeing her daddy again.

Chapter Thirty-One

They Meet

Samara was as nervous as a teenager going on her first date. The news that her father was alive and well was the best news that Samara had heard in more than year. Her world was coming to a crashing halt a few hours before, and although things still weren't looking good for her friends yet, the fact that her daddy was back would change everything.

Samara had so many questions for her father, and yet all of them were irrelevant. The only thing she needed to know was that he was alive. All she needed was to put her arms around him. She might even shed a couple of tears, although her father had forbidden her to do so. He could fuss all he wanted. She loved and missed her daddy, and if her emotions got the best of her, he would just have to deal with it. He shouldn't have been gone so damn long anyway.

According to the note she received, her father should arrive around nine in the morning, a little more than fifteen minutes away. She called Tonya's mother Sarah at the hospital to get the status on her friends. Sarah said that Tonya was still comatose, but her wounds were healing, and she had been upgraded to serious condition. Stacy was doing a lot better. She was able to get up and walk around, and Mike was set to be released that morning.

A few minutes after getting off the phone with Sarah, there came that special knock. Samara's heart pounded. Sitting in the chair about fifteen feet from the door with the AR-15 at the ready, she said, "Name."

"The pirate," the male voice responded.

"Where are you from?"

"Hell! Just visiting," he responded.

"My name."

"Sammie, also known as Little Indestructible," he said to Samara's delight. She remembered that nickname he would often call her as a kid.

"It's open. Proceed through the door very slowly."

The door opened slowly. He peeked through the door and saw his beautiful daughter and the rifle both staring him down. He saw the huge smile on her face as he entered. She tossed the rifle, ran, and jumped into her father's arms. As Rufus hugged his daughter, tears began to form in his eyes. He quickly recovered. He couldn't let his daughter see him shed any tears. However much Samara had missed her daddy, he had missed her even more.

"I love you, Daddy," Samara said while still holding on to her father. Just saying that made her feel like a little girl again. It took her back to when they spent quality time together. Sometimes it would be the movies. Other times it would be target practice out in the country. Just seeing her daddy and sharing that embrace took her back.

"I love you too, Sammie," Rufus said as they let each other go. Rufus opened the curtains to the window before sitting down on the bed. Samara went to sit beside him. He picked up her rifle and examined it. "When's the last time you cleaned this thing?"

"I haven't had a chance. Been putting in too much work," Samara said, smiling.

"That's the exact reason you should keep it well maintained. If it jams on you while you're in the middle of something, you'll wish you had cleaned it."

Samara stared at him. She rose to her feet and saluted him.

"Yes, sir," she replied, and Rufus laughed.

"How is your mother doing?" he asked.

"She's OK. You know her. Nothing really rattles her. She's just being Natalie Brown."

Rufus laughed. "I know what you mean. Does she have a boyfriend?"

Samara looked at him as if he were prying. "Daddy, Ma got married a few months ago."

The awe-filled expression on his face caused Samara to smile. She could tell that his heart was somewhere in his stomach. Samara began to laugh.

"I'm just kidding, Daddy. She's not married and doesn't have a boyfriend. How is she going to be married and still keep your last name?"

Rufus was very relieved. "I'm so glad. Your mother would have never forgiven me."

"For what?"

"For offing her husband or boyfriend. If she were involved, that temporary arrangement was set to come to an end the fast way," Rufus said as he extracted his silenced .45-caliber semi-automatic handgun. Samara's face lit up.

"You still got T-HOG? Let me see it," Samara said of the gun. Rufus passed his favorite .45 that had been nicknamed The Hand of God.

"I see she's taken some bumps and bruises," Samara said as she examined the gun.

"Good warriors usually do," he said, nodding. Samara nodded in agreement. She could definitely understand that. "She's faithful, though. Believe me, she's given much more punishment than she's taken."

"There's no doubt about that."

"How are you brothers doing?"

"Well, you know Jesse. He's doing him. Marcus is doing OK. He got shot a couple weeks ago," Samara said as Rufus's eyes widened. "It's a long story, Dad, but he's OK. His attackers are dead, though."

"I would have been more surprised if they were still alive." Rufus paused a few seconds. "You've been putting in a lot of work lately?" he asked. Samara lowered her head and nodded. "Your mother has a unique ability to see through people, a trait you obviously inherited. That being said, if you've been taking folks out, she knows about it whether you tell her or not. So what does she think about you running missions?"

"She isn't happy at all. She wants me to outsmart folks instead of killing them. She said I was acting too much like you. She said I need to get back in church and start using my brain to win." Rufus laughed hysterically. "What's so funny, Daddy?"

"I already knew that's what she told you when you said you were running missions." He stopped laughing. "She's right, too. But to your defense, if I were around, you probably would act more like her. You're like some sort of balance between us. Jesse is self-centered—the opposite of your mother. Marcus is a follower—the opposite of me. But you're the exact combination of both of us. When one of us isn't present you start to act more like the other to regain that balance, and best of all, you do it subconsciously. It's amazing."

"Daddy, you're crazy. Where have you been?"

"Now that's a long story. Basically I've been running a lot of missions and taking my share of bumps and bruises. I couldn't contact you because I think someone's looking for me and I'm not sure who. It might be another assassin. It might be hitmen from one of the foreign countries I've murdered political leaders in. It may be the mob. I really don't know, but I'm sure someone is trying to catch up with me or take me out. I was trying to make sure y'all didn't get caught up in it." He reached in his pocket. "I got something special for you," he said as he handed her some pictures.

The first picture was her at the graduation looking around for him with the binoculars. The next picture was her on the podium. The third was him in a disguise sitting beside Wayne.

"Daddy, you were there. I saw y'all, but you had on that disguise," she said as she threw the pictures on the bed and gave her dad a huge hug. "I wanted you to be there so badly."

"I was. I know how important that day was for us. They would have had to kill me to keep me away. I loved the speech, too," Rufus said. Samara was so happy that her father had made it. Rufus began to look disappointed.

"What's the matter, Daddy?"

"How do you feel about the things your daddy taught you?"

"What do you mean, Daddy?"

He looked her in the eye. "The life of an assassin."

"Maybe not for me, Daddy. It's good for me to defend myself, but not just to go around killing off my problems summarily."

Rufus began to laugh. "Do you see what I'm saying? You sound just like your mother." He stopped laughing and continued. "Lately I've been thinking the same thing. My daddy taught and told me how to become a ruthless killer, and it's been my occupation for over twenty years now. I'm ready to retire. I acquired the biggest target yet a few weeks ago and let him off the hook. It would have made my daddy proud if I would have killed him, but I didn't. I finally realized what I want in life. I want to be like Samara Brown."

"Daddy," Samara said, blushing.

"Your grandfather wanted to change the world by killing folks. After hearing your speech and hearing how you were able to help our people without murder, I knew that was what I wanted to do. Plus I need your mother back in my life." They both laughed.

"Daddy, who is Wayne? You sent him to give me the note. He was at the graduation with you. Most importantly, he looks like you in the pictures of you before I was born. Ma noticed him too and said the same thing."

"Sammie, you're pretty intelligent. You tell me."

"How old is he, Daddy?"

Rufus smiled. "I assume you know who he is?"

"I'm guessing he's a long lost sibling. How old is he, Daddy?"

"He's twenty, Samara," Rufus said. Samara was visually devastated. He was younger than her, but older than Marcus. "I cheated on your mother with a female operative I was working with. Wayne was the product of that relationship. Your mother didn't find out until years later. And even though the affair had lasted less than a year, when Natalie found out it ended our marriage. She told me there was no chance of reconciliation at the time. We decided together that we would pretend that my work as an operative was the reason our marriage had disintegrated."

Samara looked very disappointed. Rufus grasped her chin, lifting her head to face him.

"I'm sorry that it happened like that. I was a young man and let my little hormones get out of control. I never loved anyone except your mother. I didn't want to go, but she was so mad that I had an affair and a son, she couldn't see me staying. I still love your mother to this day. I hope she can forgive me one day. It's been almost fifteen years."

"What about Wayne's mother?"

"She's dead. After Wayne was born our affair ended. She was not happy about it, but there was nothing she could do about it. I was in love with your mother. If I had been man enough to admit the affair to your mother back then, maybe she would have forgiven me," Rufus said as he shook his head in disappointment. He shrugged it off. "When Wayne was about six, his mother was killed on a mission in Liberia."

"Did Ma ever meet Wayne?"

"No. She's seen pictures, but has never met him."

"Where is he now?"

"Making sure that everything is OK."

Chapter Thirty-Two

To Old Acquaintances We Forgot

An hour later Samara and Rufus were catching up on old memories and telling each other about the things that had happened since the last time they saw each other. Their reunion was a beautiful thing. The happiness that the father and daughter killers shared was one they hadn't experienced in a long time. But then their bliss was interrupted by the opening of the door.

Four white men entered the hotel room quickly. Both Rufus and Samara reached for their weapons, but were a second too late as the men already had them in their sights and fired a silenced round to warn them not to draw.

"Don't do it," a tall, burly, and balding white man warned them. The other three men holding assault rifles had their guns trained on the father and daughter. If the men decided to shoot, Samara and Rufus would have been dead before they reached their guns. Samara recognized the man who said, "Don't do it," but she didn't remember from where.

"Good morning, Mr. and Ms. Brown. I'm Special Agent Jack Simms at your service." The name Simms rang a bell with Samara. Marsha Simms was the white lady from Change for Urban America that had tried to undermine the center. Agent Simms was the same man she saw with Marsha when they had their little confrontation outside the IHOP after church. This was not looking good.

"Hey, Special Agent Simms, how's that bitch Marsha doing?" Samara asked. Rufus looked curiously at Samara, trying to figure out what was going on.

Agent Simms laughed his ass off.

"That's the most accurate description I've heard of my wife in some time. I see she's had the same effect on you that she's had on me for years." Agent Simms went over and tapped Rufus on the leg. "Hey, Rufus." He tapped him on the leg a second time, then he took a few steps back toward his cohort, who had his gun trained on Rufus's torso. "Hey, Earl, he don't like that none," Agent Simms said. "You see his face?" Earl nodded and smiled.

"Hey, Rufus, you look a little frustrated and lost, so let me bring you up to speed. My wife, Marsha Simms, under my orders made trouble for Samara and her center. Now I could give a damn about the center or your daughter, but I figured if I fucked with her enough, her daddy would show up to save the day, and here you are.

"You see, I've been trying to catch up with you for a long time now. I found out you were an army man. I tried to find out what you did after the army and found out that your file and your life were classified above my level. Since you weren't a politician or diplomat, that meant you killed people for our country. Now that, I can respect.

"But here's my problem with you, boy," Special Agent Simms said. Rufus was incensed. The fact that he wanted to kill them all, especially behind that statement, was evident by his demeanor.

"You better watch it, Jack," Earl said. "He really don't like you calling him boy."

"I saw that, Earl. If he thought he could get to his gun in time, he'd try to kill us all, too," Jack said before turning his attention back to Rufus. "I respect your skill set, boy. I hear you one of the best murderers we've produced. Not too shabby for a nigger."

Rufus closed his eyes for a second. He had to work hard to maintain his composure. He needed to calm down and figure out what the visit was about.

"So what's your problem with me, you redneck, inbred, sheep-fucking cracker?" Rufus asked. Earl and the other two gunmen were mad. Jack laughed hysterically.

"Boy, you remind me of your uncle Sam," Special Agent Simms said while watching Rufus closely. His statement shocked Rufus and Samara. Special Agent Simms liked the response he got from them. "Oh, I forgot to mention that I was born and raised in South Carolina—Greenville to be exact." Rufus looked like he had seen a ghost.

"Oh, yeah, I remember them beating the hell out of Sam and hanging him from that tree when I was a kid. But let me tell you where our destinies intertwine, boy. Your dad MC came through and murdered a couple of white men. Do you remember that? Well his second victim happened to be my dad." Neither Samara nor Rufus liked that statement. It basically ensured that they would not leave the room alive. Special Agent Simms continued.

"Now I saw your dad hang from the same tree as

your uncle. Over time I realized that wasn't good
enough for me. Since that time I've killed both of your
brothers and three of your nephews. I've been trying to
track you for a long time. After I realized that you
weren't going to be easily found, I thought your family
would be good bait. And here you are."

Rufus was in a bind. He was a killer and understood
death. He didn't mind dying. He had killed so many
people over the years that maybe it was his time. But
he could not see his daughter being killed under any
circumstances. He played on the agent's intelligence to
see where his head was concerning his daughter.

"She doesn't have anything to do with this. Let her
go on about her business," Rufus said.

Special Agent Simms gave Rufus a dumbfounded
look.

"Hey, Rufus, I tracked your daughter here. I've seen
her work. She should join the agency. I'm not into
killing women and children, but if I let her go I know
she would come back looking for me. She's not getting
a pass on this, even though I appreciate her killing off
those niggers. The less niggers in the world, the mer-
rier," Simms said. Samara was truly disgusted. "By the
way, how did you like the home makeover?" he said to
Samara. She was stunned by the revelation that the
agent had been responsible for burning down her home.

"So do you have anything else to say, boy, before we
rape, torture, and murder this fair-skinned nigger
daughter of yours?" Special Agent Simms asked.

"I do," Rufus said. He turned away from the agent
and looked out the window. He stood and waved his
hand. "Join your father," Rufus said, grabbing his
daughter as they fell on the side of the bed. Samara got
a hand out, causing both of their guns to fall with them.

A silenced shot pierced the window and hit Earl in

his forehead, dropping him instantly. As soon as they began to react a second gunman was hit in the throat. Simms dove to the ground.

"Ralph, close that damn curtain," Jack said to his only standing gunmen. "They got a damn sniper looking through that window." Ralph attempted to close the curtain, but Samara rose up and sprayed him. Simms, seeing he was in a bad situation, fired a couple shots at Samara and Rufus, and tried to slip through the door. Rufus fired two warning shots just above his head.

"Drop the gun and turn around," Rufus ordered. Simms was hesitant but knew that his refusal meant he would end up like Earl. He dropped his gun and faced them. "How you feeling there, Jack? You done killed my brothers and their boys. Threatened to rape and murder my baby girl. Jack the cracker, it's not looking good for you."

"Oh, I was just kidding, Rufus. I wasn't gonna hurt the girl," Jack said.

"Look here," Rufus said. "Seeing as how you're already dead, I'll give you one more chance at life. You and I are going to draw our weapons like cowboys. I'll give you a fighting chance," Rufus said.

"Who's to say that once I put one in your skull, your daughter or your sniper don't take me out?" Simms asked.

"My daughter is leaving. I'll close the curtains myself. It's going to be just you and me. My dad killed four white men. I've killed more than a hundred, and yet your death will be the climax of them all." He looked over to Samara. "Get out of here."

"Daddy," Samara protested with her rifle in her hand.

"Sammie," Rufus said, staring her directly in the eyes. "I said get." Feeling the weight of her father's authority, Samara walked past Jack Simms and bumped him hard in the process. Samara looked him in the eye as she exited. Jack Simms smiled after Samara bumped him. "Your daddy's a dead man. After I finish with him, I'm coming for your mother and your brothers. I'm going to kill you last," Jack said softly to Samara. She raised the gun and pointed it at his head.

"Samara!" Rufus yelled, but it was too late. Within seconds Jack knocked her gun away from him, grabbed his revolver from the small of his back, and had his gun pointed at her head, which was less than a foot away. Rufus trained his gun on Jack, but the agent slid behind Samara and held his gun to her head. Rufus smiled.

"Hey, Jack, do you know my sons' names?"

"Yeah, I know the niggers names—Jesse and Marcus Calvin, named after your dead nigger father MC."

"Let me introduce you to Wayne," Rufus said as he waved his hand. A single shot ripped through the agent's right eye, removing brain matter and skull as it passed through. Samara was relieved and scared from the bullet that killed a man less than a foot from her own head.

Rufus looked at Samara.

"So what do you think about your little brother now?" he asked.

"Little bro is all right."

Chapter Thirty-Three

Return of the Lost Sheep

Rufus went through the process of cleaning the room of any trace that he or Samara had ever been there. Fortunately for the front desk clerk who checked Samara in, she used an alias and wore a disguise, or else the clerk would have been next on the list of victims. Rufus only found FBI credentials on Simms. The other three had South Carolina IDs on them. Rufus figured they may have been the sons of the other three white men MC had put down. Simms was the only one Rufus was really concerned with.

Rufus dragged Special Agent Simms into the bathroom. He put his body into the tub, and then peeked out of the bathroom.

"Sammie, are you ready? Once I pull this pin, we're gonna have to hit these stairs hard, all the way to the garage." Samara nodded and opened the door. Rufus put Special Agent Simms's hands on his face and extracted a grenade. He put the grenade into Jack's right hand, pulled the pin, and ran. As they ran down the stairs, a violent explosion ripped through the building, jolting them. They hit the garage, got into Samara's car, and fled the building.

After traveling a couple blocks, they picked up Wayne, who stood outside an office building wearing a disguise. He tossed the large case he had in the trunk and hopped in. Samara pulled off.

Samara looked at Wayne through the rearview mirror.

"Hey, little bro," she said to Wayne. Wayne smiled.

"Hey, big sis," he replied. "You look like you're in a better mood today than the first time I met you."

"Absolutely. Thanks for saving my life back there. Well thanks for saving our lives, I should say."

"I couldn't let anything happen to my big sister. Besides, we have a lot of catching up to do. Not only do we have to get to know each other better, we have some competing to do. Dad said you were a better shot than me. I beg to differ. You've seen my work."

Samara laughed. "Anybody can hit a stationary target with a decent rifle and a scope. Let's see that shot with small arms at a range."

"That's what I'm talking about. I can't wait."

Rufus laughed. He was happy to see the camaraderie between his daughter and son, the only children he taught his ways to. For a second he thought about the damage the two of them could do by themselves. Then he thought about how powerful they could be as a family.

"Where are we headed, Daddy?" Samara asked.

"Home," Rufus replied.

"Whose home, Daddy?"

"Natalie Brown's," Rufus said to Samara's surprise.

About forty minutes later Samara, Rufus, and Wayne showed up at her mother's house. Samara had a key to the house, but for the first time since losing her key as a kid she decided to knock first. Natalie came to the door and paused. She was clearly anxious.

"Hello, Rufus," Natalie said to her estranged husband.

"Hey, Natalie. You're still looking as beautiful as ever," Rufus replied.

She ignored the comment and turned her attention to Wayne.

"Wayne?" she asked.

"Yes, Mrs. Brown," Wayne answered like a timid teenager meeting the parents of a girl he wanted to take out for the first time. Natalie came outside and gave him a big hug. Samara and Rufus were surprised by the move.

"It's a pleasure to finally meet you," Samara's mother said. "You know, you look just like your father did when he was your age."

"Yes, ma'am."

"Y'all come on in," Natalie said.

Everyone entered and made themselves comfortable in the living room. Natalie offered everyone something to drink. After getting coffee, juice, and water for her guests, she came back into the living room and sat down.

Samara told her mother about what had happened to her since leaving the hospital. She told her about the FBI agent who planned to murder them, and she explained in detail how Wayne had saved their lives. Natalie was very happy.

"You see, that's what all that foolishness is supposed to be used for, Samara and Rufus. Instead of going around killing people, you need to use those skills to stop people from being killed. It looks like the youngest of y'all three got the most sense," Natalie said.

Wayne smiled at her acknowledgement. "Where do you live, Wayne, and what do you do for a living?"

"I used to live in Chicago, but I can't go back there. I worked part-time as a staff person at a Boys and Girls Club."

"Why can't you go back there?" Wayne took a long pause before answering.

"We had some neighborhood tough guys who decided that if I wasn't with them, then I was with the police. They decided I was going to run with them or run from them. I wound up running from them after a few of the guys who tried to bully me came up missing."

Rufus and Samara looked at each other and smiled. They turned their attention to Natalie.

"You were saying," Rufus said to Natalie.

"I'll follow his lead, Ma," Samara added.

"You know, all of y'all are sick," Natalie said, and they all laughed.

"Where are my boys?" Rufus asked Natalie.

"Marcus is at the hospital helping his girlfriend recover. Jesse, well he's doing Jesse."

"As usual," Samara added. Rufus turned to Wayne.

"Jesse is the pretty-boy, ass-chaser. All he cares about is himself. Marcus, your other brother"—Samara eyed her father curiously. Rufus paused and considered his words—"Marcus is turning his life around. His big sister has him on the right path."

"I can't wait to meet them. I've known about y'all most of my life, and I'm glad I finally got the opportunity to meet you. I'm my mother's only child. It's nice to have a big sister and little brothers. I love my big sister already. She acts just like me, and I've never met her."

"That's because y'all act just like your father," Natalie interjected, and they both shrugged.

They continued conversing for about fifteen minutes until the phone rang. Natalie went to answer it.

"Hello," Natalie said. "Yes, she's right here." Natalie handed Samara the phone. "It's your brother and he says it's important." Samara was very worried. She could only assume that the bad news had to do with Tonya.

"What's up?" Samara asked.

"Mike . . . he's gone," Marcus said.

"What the hell do you mean he's gone? He was set to be discharged today. What are you talking about?"

"He's not dead. He's missing. His family was looking for him to take him home, but no one can find him. They're searching the entire building for him now."

"We're on our way," she said. "Hold on. Hey, Marcus?"

"Yeah?"

"How's Tonya doing?"

"A lot better. She came out of the coma less than an hour ago. Her mother said they haven't upgraded her status yet, though. They said it was good that she woke up. She should be fine, Samara. She's not as tough as you, but she's pretty tough for a woman. She'll be fine."

"There's no question about that. Guess who's here? Better yet, I'll let you speak to him," Samara said as she handed Rufus the phone.

"Little MC," Rufus said with a huge smile on his face.

"Dad, is that really you? I thought you were dead. I'm on my way home," MC said.

"I love you, too, son, and I'm proud of you and the changes you've made in your life. You don't have to come here. We're on our way there. I got something important to tell you, too."

"OK, Dad, I'll see you soon," Marcus said as they both hung up the phone.

"What's happened to Mike?" Samara's mother asked.

"I don't know, Ma. He was set to be discharged, but now he's just gone. He could have decided he was healthy enough to leave and just left, but I don't think he did. Something isn't right," Samara said, shaking her head.

"Enough said. Let's go, kids," Rufus said as he rose from the couch.

"Don't be taking my child—I mean children—on any missions, Rufus," Natalie said. Samara, Rufus, and Wayne were glad to hear the correction, and each smiled in turn. The change in her statement meant that Wayne was accepted into the family.

"Hey, we're just going to make sure your son-in-law is OK. We'll be gentle, OK?" Rufus asked. Natalie shook her head. The three assassins headed for the door until the phone rang again. They all stopped as Natalie answered the phone.

"Hello."

"May I speak with Samara?" a male voice asked.

"May I ask who's calling?"

"A friend of Mike's."

Natalie covered the receiver of the phone with her hand.

"It's a man who says he's a friend of Mike's. He wants to talk with Samara." Samara immediately grabbed the phone.

"This is Samara. Who is this?" Samara asked. There was silence. "Who is this?"

"Samara, you've been a bad girl and have caused me

a lot of problems. I have your faggot-ass boyfriend right here. The boys have been using him as a human punching bag for the last thirty minutes. At the rate of blood he's losing, and those lumps upside his head, it doesn't look good for him. This is what you need to do. I have a couple of friends in a car outside of your mother's house. Come on and take a ride with them. Let's talk. I promise you'll see Mike alive."

Samara put down the phone and looked out the window. Her father and brother followed suit. Samara saw a Cadillac Escalade with dark tinted windows idling in front of the house. She walked back over to the phone.

"How about I just go and murder everyone in the truck?" Samara asked.

"Well that's certainly an option, but then I'll just murder your boyfriend and go pick up one of your brothers, have some fun with them. Maybe pick up your mother later. I'm gonna see you, Samara. Just come and see me now and I'll give everyone else a pass. Oh, yeah, and leave your guns at home. We wouldn't want anybody to get hurt."

Chapter Thirty-Four

Samara rode in the back of the Escalade with a man on each side. Her hands and mouth were duct taped. The man in the passenger seat routinely turned around to point a gun in her face and warn her about making any hasty moves. The slang he used reminded her of Craig and other New York natives.

"Hey, ma, you fine as hell. I hope they are wrong about you. You and I needs to get acquainted and shit," one of the men beside her said. Samara mumbled, the duct tape stifling her words. The man beside her removed the duct tape. "What'd you say?"

"What do they think about me?" Samara asked.

The man in the passenger seat turned around and flashed his gun in her face again.

"That you're a dead woman," he responded.

"You keep pointing that gun at me, and you'll be going first." Everyone in the truck laughed.

"She must be the one that did it," the guy sitting beside her said, and then he replaced the duct tape.

"You're real tough right now," the man in the passenger seat replied. "We'll see if you're so tough when I put this dick to you in front of your boyfriend."

Samara knew that she was in serious trouble. She had a good idea of what was planned for her after they didn't blindfold her. They didn't care if she saw their faces because she wouldn't be able to tell anyone once she was dead. It was cool, though, because all of her cards weren't on the table yet.

"Hey, yo," the driver said, slowing down and looking in his rearview mirror.

"What's up?" the guy in the passenger seat asked.

"This car has been trailing us through the last three turns. It stays pretty far back, but I keep seeing the motherfucker. I think they're following us," the driver replied.

"Pull over and see what they do."

"Pull over? It could be the fucking vice. I'm not pulling over," the driver said.

"Well slow down at the next light until it turns yellow, then speed through it," the front seat passenger said as the back seat passengers looked very nervous.

The driver did as he was told, speeding through the yellow light. By the time the car reached the intersection the light was red, and the cross traffic had already entered the intersection. The truck sped ahead and made a right.

"I lost them," the driver proclaimed. And now Samara was the one looking nervous.

About ten minutes later they arrived at an old, abandoned warehouse just off of New York Avenue in Northeast. They waited a couple of minutes before they got out, making sure that the car that followed them hadn't found them. There was no sign of the car. Everyone got out and headed into the building.

"We goin' have a good old time," the man who was riding in the front passenger's seat said as he grabbed her ass.

They entered into a large two-story room. In the middle of the floor, Mike sat tied up to a chair, badly beaten and semi-conscious. There was a man who stood in front of him. He punched him the face as Samara entered. She broke free and tried to run over to help him, but was tackled about fifteen feet short of her goal. There was another chair beside Mike, and Samara was placed in it.

A well-dressed, tall black man in his early forties entered the room. He walked over to Samara and Mike.

"Y'all watch the perimeter," the man said, dismissing the four men who had brought her there. "Hello, Samara Brown," the well-dressed man said, finally turning his attention to his new captive. Samara recognized the voice as the man who had called her mother's house. "My name is Joe. This is Murda," he said of the man who had struck Mike as Samara entered. "I'll explain to you why you're here, and then I'll remove the tape to see what you have to say.

"My godson's name is Craig," Joe said. Samara's eyes got wide. "Yeah, your ex-boyfriend is my godson. He was taking care of business down here for me. I told him that he didn't have to sell drugs anymore because he was headed to the NBA. In fact, I stopped selling drugs to him. Unfortunately my son Joe Jr. saw a gold mine down here and continued to sell to Craig."

Samara really didn't like where this conversation was headed. Every other statement Joe made reaffirmed her belief that she and Mike wouldn't leave the room alive. The worst part about the situation was that the Escalade managed to elude her backup plan. If her father and brother didn't miraculously find them soon, they would only find their dead bodies.

"See, Joe Jr. and his man T-Dog were two of the three people you killed while you were trying to take out Craig. What I don't understand was how you killed three armed men, and Craig, by far the least violent of the four, was the only one to survive? Did you still have feelings for him and let him off the hook? How is it that he survived?" Joe asked, but of course Samara remained silent because her mouth was still taped.

"He was in police custody at the hospital. We had a nurse help spring him loose the same way we got your boyfriend. I hear his man from down here named Toni was an informant. They've been watching Craig for months. I had to murder my godson to make sure he didn't start snitching. It's all very sad. I wish he had gone to Syracuse or some other school closer to home. Now all of this blood has been shed because he liked Howard's homecoming parties," Joe said as he shook his head. He removed the tape from her mouth. "Do you have any last words?"

"What does Mike have to do with this? He wasn't with me when I murdered those chumps. Why don't you let him go?" Samara asked.

"Maybe he was, maybe he wasn't. But it's hard for me to believe you could have done all of that damage by yourself. Either way, someone I loved was killed. Therefore, someone you love is going to die. My question still stands. Do you have any last words?"

"What are you going to do, shoot us in the head?"

"Maybe, but I was thinking more along the lines of multiple stab wounds and throat slitting."

"How about this, Joe?" Samara asked. "You seem like a fair, but ruthless old timer. Let me and Murda fight head up. If I win, you let Mike go. If I lose, we both get it." Joe shrugged.

"I'm up for a little entertainment. What you say, Murda?"

"Are you serious?" Murda asked Joe, and then he turned to Samara. "OK. As long you understand that once I beat that ass, I'm taking it. I'm gonna fuck you right in front of your man. I might fuck him, too."

"We'll see about that," Samara replied.

Joe took a couple steps back and extracted a Desert Eagle semi-automatic, high powered handgun.

"If you think about running, it won't be me or Murda chasing you. It will be these fifty cals."

Murda began to remove the ropes that bound Samara to the chair. Samara thought she had a pretty good shot at taking Murda, although he was buff like he had just gotten out of prison. It really didn't matter either way. She needed to stall her and Mike's deaths for as long as possible. She was hoping that her brother and father would find them. She needed to give that possibility as much time as she could.

The second he removed the duct tape from her wrists she punched him in the nose. The blow caught him by surprise and temporarily stunned him, more out of surprise and irritation than from pain. She followed up with a forearm and elbow across his chin that caused the big man to stumble. Samara took a glance over at Joe, who looked really amused but still had that DE at his side. He was about fifteen feet away. If she tried to make a move on him from that distance, it would've been fatal.

It suddenly hit Samara that Murda probably had a gun too. When she turned her attention back to him, Murda suddenly hit Samara. The blow sent Samara sprawling across the floor. Unfortunately she was still about ten feet away from Joe. Murda came over to put in more work. As he stood over her, Samara kicked him in the nuts. He clutched his privates and doubled over in pain.

"Murda, you didn't see that coming?" Joe asked, shaking his head.

Samara quickly got off the ground and grabbed the back of his head, causing it to collide with her knee. Murda fell back and hit his head on the floor. He rolled over in pain.

"Oh, this is ridiculous," Joe said. He raised his gun and pointed it at Samara. "Go sit back in your seat." Samara complied.

"Can I release my man?" she asked.

"I'm about to release him, and send you both on your way—straight to hell."

Suddenly there was commotion outside. Gunshots rang out and Joe began to look very anxious. He moved over to help Murda off the ground while facing Samara the entire time. As Joe tried to help his partner up a single bullet caused his head to explode. Rufus and Wayne walked casually into the room like nothing had happened. Murda was completely paralyzed with fear. As Rufus and Wayne casually strolled over toward Samara, Rufus shot Murda in the face while continuing to look at his daughter and walk toward her. Rufus and Wayne released Mike.

"You see that, sis?" Wayne asked. "I scored a head shot from twenty yards away with a .44. You don't got skills like those. I'll teach you about that some day." Samara looked at Rufus, and then back at Wayne.

"It was a good shot, a damn good shot. You still aren't on my level, but you're pretty good," Samara said with a smile.

Epilogue

The Beginning

About a week later the center had a big celebration during Labor Day weekend. Everyone was at the center including Stacy, Marcus, Natalie, Rufus, Wayne, and Mike. Tonya was the only person absent. She was still at the hospital, but she was in much better shape. She was up and walking around, and doing extensive rehabilitation.

Samara was laughing and joking with the kids when Lieutenant Snow entered the center. He made a beeline for Samara.

"Can I talk with you outside for a moment?" he asked Samara. She agreed and accompanied him outside. He handed her a notice.

"What the hell is this?" Samara asked before looking at the document. After reading it she said, "An arrest warrant? You've got to be kidding me!" Lieutenant Snow smiled. "What are you arresting me for?"

"Read the warrant," he said.

"Suspect in a triple homicide? You can't be serious."

"Oh, I was. Either you're the luckiest person I've

"Whatever," Wayne replied.

"We could use your skills at the center," Samara said. Rufus and Wayne looked confused. "Not your shooting skills. You said you worked for the Boys and Girls Club up in Chicago. Our community center is like that, but we're just a lot more involved in the community. Do you want the job?"

"Absolutely," Wayne said. He came over and gave his sister a hug.

"What about me?" Rufus asked. His children came over and gave him a hug. "I'm not talking about a hug. I told you I'm retiring. I need a job at the center, too." They all laughed.

"Sure, Dad, but we need to get away from here and fast," Samara said. They helped Mike to his feet. "Hey, baby, this is my dad, Rufus. And that's my little brother, Wayne. Dad and little bro, this is Mike."

"Hey, Mike," they said in unison.

"Hey, Mr. Brown and Wayne. I didn't plan on meeting y'all like this," Mike replied through swollen lips and a partially disfigured face.

"Yeah, you were about ten seconds from never meeting them at all," Samara added.

"I love you, Maury," Mike said. Samara blushed.

"I love you, too, Michael McMillan."

come across, or the best. Our star witness was murdered. Do you know anything about that?"

"I can't say that I do. I did hear a dead man talking about another dead man, but you can't really trust them, you know," Samara said.

"So you're just going to rub it in, huh?" Samara smiled. "I'll be the bigger person and admit that you won. You're pretty good at your game. I'll give you that. So according to our bet, I'm on your side. If there is anything I can do, let me know."

"Are you going to help me hang that damn councilman?" Samara asked.

"He's hung himself. You don't need my help for that. Besides, I'm not fighting your fights for you. You do a good job of that on your own. I'm only here to help you."

"You thought you had me with that triple, didn't you?" Samara asked as the lieutenant nodded in agreement and started to walk away. "Oh, yeah, tell Deidre I said hi," Samara called out. Lieutenant Snow turned around, amazed by what he had heard. He shook his head and began to walk away, but then returned.

"Samara, I like you a lot. Thinking about it, I'm kind of glad that you won. It shows that you have the resilience to fight this fight. You see, you've stepped over a minor obstacle in a major uphill battle. You're trying to change a world that doesn't like change. Most people who try to spark a revolution don't die of old age or natural causes.

"When you take this program across the nation and it's seen as a movement, it will also be seen as a threat. I wish you success, but that success won't be coming easy. Stick in there, young buck. You'll be all right."

"There's no question about that. Like most revolutionaries, I'm willing to do for what I believe in. If I can spark the imagination of a few, then the fight continues. I'll liken the demise of The System to the Fall of Rome. There's going to be lengthy, sustained attacks and uprisings. And it may take a long time, but this empirical, racist, and unjust system shall fall."

Lieutenant Snow smiled. "I hear you, Hannibal. Like I said, I'm in your corner. Do what you gotta do, because they're not going to make it easy for you," the lieutenant reiterated and began to walk away again.

"Lieutenant Snow," Samara called to him. He turned to face her. "Fuck 'em. They don't have to make it easy for me. I plan on making it hard for them." With that they both smiled and went their separate ways.

About the Author

A DC native who still works and lives in "Da City," D. is the new voice of Black Literature. After graduating from a highly esteemed arts school, D. furthered his education by learning life lessons on the mean streets of the city. After years of trials, tribs, and procrastination, he has put his writing back at the top of his priorities with his debut novel, *Chaos in the Capital City*. He is currently at work on his next book.

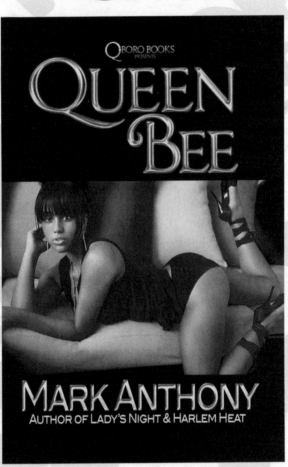

AVAILABLE
DECEMBER 2008

Black Diamond proves why some details are meant to be kept secret. The result of simple pillow talk will leave two best friends fighting to survive.